THE UNSUSPECTED

CHARLOTTE
ARMSTRONG

Introduction by
OTTO PENZLER

AMERICAN
MYSTERY
CLASSICS

Penzler Publishers
New York

This is a work of fiction. Names, characters, places, and incidents either are the product of the author's imagination or are used fictitiously. Any resemblance to actual persons, living or dead, businesses, companies, events, or locales is entirely coincidental.

Published in 2019 by Penzler Publishers
58 Warren Street, New York, NY 10007
penzlerpublishers.com

Distributed by W. W. Norton

Cover image: Andy Ross
Cover design: Mauricio Diaz

Paperback ISBN 9781613161234
Hardcover ISBN 9781613161227
eBook ISBN 9781453245736

Library of Congress Control Number: 2018963376

Printed in the United States of America

9 8 7 6 5 4 3 2 1

OTTO PENZLER PRESENTS
AMERICAN MYSTERY CLASSICS

THE UNSUSPECTED

Charlotte Armstrong (1905-1969) was an American poet, dramatist, and author of mystery short stories and novels. She was born and raised in the mining region of Michigan's Upper Peninsula. After two years at the University of Wisconsin, she moved to New York and received a B.A. degree from Barnard in 1925. She had two plays produced on Broadway but neither was successful, so she turned to writing mystery fiction, beginning with *Lay On, MacDuff* (1942), the first of three detective novels featuring Professor MacDougal Duff. It was with *The Unsuspected* that she achieved outstanding success and moved to Hollywood while it was being filmed. The 1947 Warner Brothers feature starred Claude Rains, Joan Caulfield, Audrey Totter, and Hurd Hatfield; it was directed by Michael Curtiz.

Otto Penzler, the creator of American Mystery Classics, is also the founder of the Mysterious Press (1975), a literary crime imprint now associated with Grove/Atlantic; MysteriousPress.com (2011), an electronic-book publishing company; and New York City's Mysterious Bookshop (1979). He has won a Raven, the Ellery Queen Award, two Edgars (for the *Encyclopedia of Mystery and Detection*, 1977, and *The Lineup*, 2010), and lifetime achievement awards from NoirCon and *The Strand Magazine*. He has edited more than 70 anthologies and written extensively about mystery fiction.

THE UNSUSPECTED

INTRODUCTION

Charlotte Armstrong was a hard-working and talented writer across a wide spectrum of genres, including journalism, poetry, drama, and mystery fiction. Born and raised in Vulcan, an iron-mining town on Michigan's Upper Peninsula, in 1897, she spent two years at the University of Wisconsin before moving to New York City, where she earned her Bachelor of Arts degree from Barnard in 1925. After working in an office for a brief time, she became a fashion reporter until marrying advertising executive Jack Lewi in 1928.

After marriage, the Lewis settled in New Rochelle, where, while raising their three children, Armstrong honed her craft and experimented with writing in various forms. She wrote poetry that was published in *The New Yorker*; she wrote plays, inspired by her work with local high school students in a small theater, and had two produced on Broadway; eventually, she tried her hand at writing mystery fiction. While her poetry and plays achieved modest success—*The Happiest Day* (1939) and *Ring Around Elizabeth* (1941) ran for seven and ten performances respectively—her mystery writing caught on much more quickly. Beginning with *Lay On, MacDuff* (1942), Armstrong wrote three consecutive detective novels featuring Professor MacDougal Duff.

She then turned to writing stand-alones. With her fourth title, the suspense novel *The Unsuspected* (1946), originally serialized in the *Saturday Evening Post*, Armstrong finally enjoyed widespread popularity as well as critical accolades. The book was a success on every count, even if it was controversial: while reviewers generally praised the quality of the writing and the skill of the author, some criticized the story's unorthodox structure, which revealed the murderer's identity almost at the outset of the story. Still, even those critics had to concede that the book's suspense was not diminished at all by this structure, and had they known more about the long tradition of the mystery novel at the time, they may have recognized antecedents that showed Armstrong's writing as part of a lineage, and not, as was claimed, a rejection of narrative norms.

This, of course, was before *Columbo*, one of the most successful television shows of all time, which made a commonplace element of suspense fiction the challenge of discovering where the culprit went wrong and how he would be caught. But long before *Columbo* or *The Unsuspected*, R. Austin Freeman, one of the giants of the British Golden Age, became famous for having invented this type of plot, known as the inverted detective story. Between Freeman and Armstrong, many others had written in this same style, including Anthony Berkeley Cox, Freeman Wills Croft, and Dorothy L. Sayers.

Controversy or no, the book was a hit, and when Hollywood bought the rights, Armstrong and her family moved to Southern California for the filming and decided to stay, taking up residence in Glendale.

The 1947 film adaptation was directed by Michael Curtiz for Warner Brothers soon after his great successes with *Casablanca* and *Mildred Pierce*. Although the storyline took a great number of liberties with the novel, it was well-received and was enhanced by an excellent cast that included Claude Rains, Joan Caulfield, and Audrey Totter.

The film version veered from the book's plot to some degree, transforming the novel into a noir film. It is largely remembered today for a single, characteristically noir scene in which a blackmailed man tries unsuccessfully to drown out his violent thoughts in a dark hotel room; as his window frames the neon sign for the establishment, "HOTEL PEEKSKILL," in a way that perfectly isolates the letters "KILL," his solace is instead assaulted by the flashing word that pries at his darkest thoughts.

The move to Hollywood allowed Armstrong to devote her full attention to writing, giving rise to a period of unusual prolificity for the author, during which she produced numerous short stories, novelettes, and more than twenty additional novels. She also wrote television scripts, including several that were produced by Alfred Hitchcock.

Suspense and peril to the young and the elderly are the characteristics of the Charlotte Armstrong mystery, and never more powerfully than in *Mischief* (1950), which featured a psychopathic babysitter. The novel became the basis for the rather dark film *Don't Bother to Knock* (1952), which starred Richard Widmark, Marilyn Monroe, and Anne Bancroft.

Armstrong has been described as the leading moralist in the mystery writing community, with a profound understanding of the psychology of individuals and of groups of ordinary people, mainly eschewing an examination of the abnormal psychology that so fascinated such authors as Margaret Millar and Patricia Highsmith. Her characters are sane, decent people who find themselves in difficult situations or are trying to protect the innocent, and who emerge triumphant because their fundamental decency will defeat the evil antagonists with whom they battle.

Charlotte Armstrong was nominated for six Edgar Allan Poe

awards (three times for best novel, three times for best short story), winning for best novel in 1957 for *A Dram of Poison. The Unsuspected* was selected as one of the best mystery novels of all time by Howard Haycraft and Frederic Dannay (half of the Ellery Queen writing team) in their "Definitive Library of Detective-Crime-Mystery Fiction."

—Otto Penzler

1

On a February Monday, in the afternoon, too late for lunch, too early for tea, the restaurant was nearly empty. A party of stout "girls" were quarreling over the check with high-pitched, playful cries. Two men at another table were eating very fast and swapping manly gossip.

A blond girl in a powder-blue suit was waiting in the lobby. She was a butter-and-eggs, sugar-and-cream kind of girl, with yellow hair, pink-and-white skin, round blue eyes. Her small nose, snubbed up at the end, might have been drawn by an illustrator of children's books. She was cute.

The man who came in very fast through the revolving door might have been roughly classified as tall, dark and handsome. He was muscular and a trifle too thin for his expensive suit. His face had a bleak and guarded expression. The girl in blue got up. They were not alike. You wouldn't have guessed from their meeting that they were blood relatives. But if you had watched them wisely you would have known them to be close in understanding, and that she was anxious about him.

She put her hand on his sleeve. "Let's get us a corner."

The man's face loosened a little. "How are you, Jane?"

"All right."

There were plenty of empty corners. They found a table against the partition that bounded the bar. "No uniform any more," she commented.

The man didn't answer. He looked across the big room with all the clean white tablecloths. It was very warm and dim and quiet, with soft music coming over the radio in the bar behind them. He looked down at five different kinds of spoons. His left hand massaged the familiar ache in his right forearm.

Jane said, "I had to see you. I was afraid you'd go up there."

"Up to Dedham, Connecticut? Why would I go up there?" He drew a breath. He didn't want to talk about it. He had hoped she wouldn't talk about it. He said, "She isn't even buried there."

"No," said Jane.

"She's dead."

"Yes."

"And that's that." She began to murmur something, but he said, "How've you been?"—warning her off.

"All right," said Jane again. She had picked up her purse and was holding it tightly with both hands. "Did Rosaleen write you often, Fran?"

"Of course she wrote." He moved his shoulders impatiently.

"What are you thinking?"

"I thought maybe," he said, "we could meet and have a bite without—"

Jane said, "You're the only one I can talk to."

"Then don't ask foolish questions," he said unhappily. "You know what I'm thinking. Naturally, I'm wondering why. Why?" He spread both hands flat on the table, as if he were going to push it aside and get up and leave. "If you know why, then you can tell me and get it over. Why did Rosaleen want to die so much that she had to hang herself?" He got it out brutally. It was what he was thinking.

Jane's pretty face began to look pinched, as if she were cold. Francis leaned back against the seat. "I want to understand it," he said more quietly. "And I'm prepared to understand it. Go ahead. And if you've got to go gently," he sighed, "I guess I can stand it."

"I've got to go slow," she said, a bit stubbornly. "Rosaleen wrote me a letter." She opened her bag and took out the letter. He could see Rosaleen's pretty handwriting, sloping back and running a little uphill.

"I don't want to read it, Jane."

"All right." She put the letter down on the tablecloth. "I don't want you to do anything but listen to me a few minutes. Fran, could you try . . . not to wince away so much?"

He didn't answer, but he relaxed a little. He knew she wouldn't talk about it just to hurt him. She began with care.

"Rosaleen must have written you about her job—about Luther Grandison, didn't she?"

"That's her boss."

"You know who he is?"

"Sure. I know. He was a director for the stage and the movies, wasn't he? The one who did all those wonderful melodramas years ago? Wrote a book of memoirs—famous guy."

"Yes," said Jane. "Well—" She picked up her fork and put it into the creamed chicken.

"So Rosaleen fell in love with her boss," said Francis.

Jane's fingers opened and the fork fell. "No, no, no! Lord, he's more than sixty! He's an ugly old man! He's not like that. That isn't it at all."

"What then?"

She didn't answer. She was looking at him as if she'd had a glimpse of the fantastic regions of his mind.

"Look, Janey, I said I was prepared to understand, but you don't seem to get it. I simply mean that it's been a long time and I realize what time can do. Rosaleen's been in the back of my life, the back of my mind—the back of my heart, if you want to put it that way—ever since I can remember. We were kids. We were cousins. Everybody paired us off in the old days. But time's gone by and we've been apart, and maybe she grew up and changed. What I'm trying to tell you is that if she did change and got mixed up emotionally—"

"But she hadn't changed," Jane said. "She hadn't changed at all."

Well then, he thought, the girl who had died still was Rosaleen, unchanged. Little and dark and tense and vivid. Her heels tapped quickly across a remembered room. The way she walked, the way she turned her head, the straight set of her shoulders, her pale skin, her black hair, her red dresses and her thin red mouth were alive again.

He forced his eyes to focus. "Then why?" he burst "Then why did she do it?"

Jane put her hand on his fist "No reason."

"No—"

"There simply wasn't anything," she said. "Now sit still, Fran. This is what I've got to tell you: First, there was something in this letter. I'll show you in a minute. Cousin Hilda had to go up there to Dedham and get—bring her—bring the body back. There wasn't anyone else to do it. Geoffrey was down in bed, sick. You were overseas. Buddy's gone. So of course I went too. All the time on the train Hilda kept saying she couldn't understand, she couldn't understand. That's what I thought you'd say. You know as well as we do how Rosaleen believed in everything. She was even—well, religious in a way, wouldn't you say? And not a bit afraid. She always stood right up to everything. She just couldn't have done it! That's what Cousin Hilda said. And I felt that too. There are some things you can't believe, even when they happen."

"Go on," he said tonelessly.

"When the train pulled in, I saw him out the window. This Luther Grandison. He was out there on the platform. I took one look, and he was kind of . . . stagy! Standing there, looking tragic, and people all around, watching him! Fran, it made me mad! I had the feeling somebody'd written the script I—" Jane stopped.

He said gently, "What did you do?"

"I had a brainstorm. I told Cousin Hilda to pretend I hadn't come. And I went up to him after the services and asked for Rosaleen's job. I got it, Fran. I'm Grandison's secretary. He doesn't know I ever knew her. I'm Miss Moynihan."

He said, "Why?"

Jane said violently, "Because I hate him! I want you to listen. He talks on the air at four o'clock. He's a guest."

He had turned on the bench to look down on her. He seemed calm and detached. "So you hate Luther Grandison. What's it got to do with Rosaleen?"

Jane hesitated. "You know how she . . . did it, don't you? And you know she left a note? You know what it said?"

"Hilda put the clipping in her letter." His voice was flat.

"Didn't you think it was funny she didn't mention a name of any of us, even you?"

"I thought it sounded sick," said Francis. "And religious, maybe."

"You know she didn't sign it?" He moved his shoulders. "Fran, I found that note!"

"You found it?"

"I mean I found the text of it, in a book."

He kept looking at her, and his scalp seemed to lift and settle, his face changed. "Go on."

"It was copied out in her handwriting, but, Francis, it was copied. Out of an old book of trials in Scotland. One of those old cases. You know, he's kind of an authority on murder."

"Murder?" said Francis.

His voice was light and rather gentle. They were the only customers in the whole room now. The soft music from the bar was punctuated by the click of silver, off in a corner, where a busboy was sorting it away.

Francis was thinking. Murder. One person dead, that meant. He'd seen them die in quantities, seen the flames come up like an answer from the earth beneath. Yet when it was just one, alone, that was murder. There was something a little bit quaint and out of joint in the mixed values.

Jane said, "What shall I do?"

Francis picked up a spoon and balanced it on his finger. "You think Rosaleen was murdered?" He might have been asking, Do you think it's going to rain? "By whom?" he said.

"By Luther Grandison."

All he said, again, was, "Why?"

"Read the letter."

He took up the letter; his eyes raced through. Stuff about the weather, kidding stuff about Jane and Buddy. "Who is Tyl?" His voice was different; suddenly it had become crisp and demanding.

"Tyl's Mathilda. One of Grandison's wards. He has two—two girls. They lived there with him most of the time."

"Who's Althea?"

"That's the other one—the beautiful one. She's married to Oliver Keane now. Look."

Jane's finger pointed out the paragraph Rosaleen had written in her breezy style:

> The old spider makes out like money's too, too vulgar, but he had his reasons why he'd rather marry off Althea. Some day I'll tell you what makes me say that. It makes me mad. He's so smooth and philosophical, you tend to get fooled. The last

thing on earth you'd imagine would be what I'm . . . imagining! Sorry, hon. Let it go until I see you.

But her pen had refused to leave the subject. The scrawl went angrily on:

Nobody can tell me money's not like the blood in his veins! And if he's so wise, why doesn't he know that Tyl's heart is broken? Because it's broken, Jane, a real smash! And that's an awful thing to be in the same house with. She's going away, thank God. And Oliver's moving in.

I think he does know it's broken! I don't think he cares! I think he is perfectly selfish! I think— Sorry, I'm in a bad mood. I feel like throwing things. Excuse it, please, and love.

YOUR ROSALEEN.

"Well?" said Francis coolly.

Jane said eagerly, tumbling the story out, "Matilda was the rich one—very, very rich. Her parents both got killed in the same accident when she was a little girl. Her father lived just long enough to turn her and all the money over to Grandison. And it was Mathilda that Oliver Keane was engaged to. And only two days before their wedding, he went and married the other one."

"Althea?"

"Yes, Althea Conover, and she's not rich at all. Of course, she's gorgeous, and I guess poor Mathilda wasn't so hot. Althea's the daughter of another friend. Grandy took her in."

"Grandy?"

"That's what the girls call him. Now, here's the thing, Fran. This is the way Mathilda's money was fixed. She was to make her own will at twenty-one, and she did. But she didn't get the money then. She was to get control whenever she married! Don't you see?"

"No," said Francis.

"Grandy didn't want her to get married. So there must have been something funny about the money."

He shook his head.

"I don't care," she insisted. "What if he'd done something he shouldn't? What if Rosaleen did find out? She'd bring it right out in the open. You know she would. She wouldn't have stopped to think to be afraid. So, you see?"

"He killed her because she knew too much," said Francis, and began to laugh. It was pretty rusty laughter.

Jane said, "I'll give up the job and go home, if you say so." Jane's tea was cold. "Just the same," she said, "if Rosaleen felt like throwing things, that's not a suicidal mood."

Francis' face darkened. He looked at the date on the letter. "So a man of over sixty took hold of a lively little dame like Rosaleen Wright and hung her up by the neck? And she just quietly let him? Come, Jane."

"It's a soundproof room."

"It is?" he said.

"He could have talked the noose around her neck," said Jane bitterly. "The man can talk!" She looked at her watch.

"But hanging!" he burst out. "Why not poison? Why not—"

Jane broke open a hard roll. "If the note he got her to copy happens to talk about hanging, as it did, then maybe he thought it had better be hanging." She put butter on the roll and then put the roll down on her plate and pushed the plate away. She put her fingertips to her temples. "I'm not trying to believe this. If you really think I'm crazy, Fran, I wish you'd tell me so."

He said, "Honey, I don't know."

The waiter was getting nervous. Those two. They didn't eat. Now they weren't even talking. The man had looked kinda sad and tired when they came in, but now— Cripes, the guy was boiling. Whatever she told him, it sure made him mad. The waiter went over and got himself a drink of water, watching over the brim of the glass.

Jane whimpered, "I wish I hadn't said anything. Now I've got you upset, and what's the use?"

Francis turned his head and brought himself back. He'd been thinking, when they killed yours you killed them. That's the way it was in the war. But this was going to be different. He knew he had to get the anger swallowed under, and think about proof and stuff like that, think legal. Move slowly. Be sure. Put it in the department of the brain.

"Find out," he said aloud.

"The trouble is, I don't see how," said Jane. "Fran, I know there's something wrong. I know it as I know I've got a hole in the heel of my stocking, where it doesn't show. First I guessed and then I wondered, but the longer I'm up there in that house, the better I know it! I feel it! I smell it! And still I can't see what to do."

Francis beckoned and the waiter came sidling over. "Take this junk away and bring us sandwiches and coffee. Any kind."

"First you think, 'Go to the police,'" Jane was saying. "All right. With what will we go to the police? I've thought and thought—"

"Walk in," he murmured, "and say, 'I'm Miss Wright's fiancé. I don't think she committed suicide. I think she was murdered.'"

Jane nodded. "They'd say, 'Why?'"

"Naturally. So I say, 'Well, she didn't compose her own suicide note.'" He frowned.

"But they say," Jane took it up, "'Who did it?' And you say, 'Why, that nationally known figure, Mr. Luther Grandison, the famous director, the man who staged *Dead Men Do Talk* with Lillian Jellico in 1920.'" She looked at her wrist. "Oh, quick, we're missing it. Tell him to ask the bartender. The radio. I want you to hear Grandison."

"You know what he's going to say?"

"Of course I do. But I want you to hear."

Francis hailed a busboy, and Jane gave the message. Francis said, "Where were we? The police were laughing."

"Oh, they'd be laughing, all right," said Jane. "We say, 'We think he might have stolen some money from a ward of his, and his secretary found out and might have been threatening to expose him.' Then they laugh fit to die. They'd say, 'But Mr. Grandison made a lot of money in the theater before he retired. And in the movies. And his book.' They'd say, 'Prove it.'"

"Yeah," said Francis. His eyes had a kind of light behind them or deep within. "How are we going to prove it?"

"Well, there's a lawyer," said Jane wearily, "who comes up once in a while. He takes care of everything. Grandy doesn't. I write all the checks to pay the house bills. Grandy signs them without even looking. He won't talk about money. He won't look at figures. He pretends it's all so vulgar and distressing; says it affects his digestion. Says life should simply flow."

"Does he talk like that?"

"Oh, lordy, lordy, you have no idea how he talks."

"I've read his—"

Jane put up her hand. "Listen." The bartender had changed stations on the radio. Music was cut off. Instead, there was a voice. Jane's hand came down and her fingers fastened on his wrist. The place was quiet enough so that they could hear clearly. It was easy to hear and to understand that persuasive voice. If you began to listen, it caught you. It wove a musical snare for your attention, and then it spun a web of words to hold you, smooth words that came pouring without effort, pouring forth, delicately inflected, persuasive, fascinating.

"How many masks do we meet in a day?" the voice was saying. The cadences were full of regret and wonder, and a little relish. "How many ordinary human faces, two eyes, a nose and a mouth?

The man on the bus, the clerk behind the counter, each has a secret. And there are some whose secret is not innocent, but who must wear their masks until they die. I call them The Unsuspected."

Jane's nails went into the flesh on Francis' wrist.

"I myself know such a man." This was Luther Grandison speaking. This was his voice. "Yes, I know a man who has committed that gravest and most interesting of all crimes, the crime of murder, and who never has been suspected at all. No, he lives, and has lived for years, wearing his mask, taken for one of us, ordinary, going about his daily business, and yet he did it! I say, he did it!" The voice fell. "I say I know. I had better add that the authorities also know. But alas, such knowing is not legal proof." The voice was so sorry. It was sorry about everything, but faintly pleased too.

"You see, with all our cleverness, we do not know how to tear the mask from his face. And, indeed, were I to give his name, he might use the law itself to punish me for what he would call libel. And yet"—in a thrilling whisper—"he did it!"

A beat of silence. Then the voice said softly, and it licked its chops with relish now, "Oh, they are among us. The Unsuspected! There's many a murder, not only unsolved but unheard of, unknown . . . unknown. You may be sure, men and women have gone to their graves, quietly assisted, with no fuss and no bother."

The voice died. It left its audience with that delicious little shudder that Luther Grandison knew how to give them. His famous trick of putting terror into the commonplace. It was like the little touches in his plays, the Grandison touches, in which he took the ordinary, and gave it just a little flip, and it was terrifying.

Jane opened her eyes. "That's Grandy. You see?"

Francis sat still with angry white face. "The Unsuspected," he murmured. "Has he got the crust to mean himself?"

2

"SUPPOSE I go to see this lawyer?" His voice was sharp and angry.

"You can't walk in there and say, 'Look, folks, I want to see all the dope on the Frazier fortune.'"

"The law could."

"The law won't!" she wailed. "He's unsuspected. And, Fran, if you try to stir up something that way, I can see what would happen. He'd be ever so gentle with you. But he'd treat you like a museum piece. He'd put you in his collection of psychopaths. By the time he got through, everybody would be so sorry for the poor young fiancé, unbalanced by grief."

"Like that, eh?" The rich purr of Grandy's voice hung remembered between them. "Well, let that go for a minute," snapped Francis. "Start another way. How did he do it?"

"He's even got an alibi," said Jane despairingly. "Althea was with him. I mean, she saw Rosaleen alive, and after that Grandy was with her all the time, until they found—"

"Althea saw her?"

"Well, heard her speak, anyway."

Francis' eyes lit again. "What if we could show the alibi's a fake?"

"If we could! Fran, do you think a private detective—"

Francis let his lips go into something like a smile. "I think I'll attend to this myself," he said.

Jane moaned. She took hold of his hand, but he twisted it around and patted hers reassuringly. "We're going to have to assume he did it," he said in a moment. "Because if he really did, in fact, in cold blood, then this Grandison is dangerous."

Jane agreed. "He's dangerous."

The waiter came with their new order. Francis bit into the sandwich. They were both hungry, suddenly.

"Could I get at those girls?" he asked her.

"Mathilda's drowned," said Jane, with her mouth full.

"She's what? How?"

Jane read his mind. "Oh, no, Grandy couldn't have had anything to do with it. She started out for Bermuda and the ship went down—oh, five weeks ago. They haven't heard a thing since."

"So she's drowned. That's the rich one?"

"Uh-huh."

"She was lost before this happened to Rosaleen?"

"Uh-huh."

"Who gets her dough?"

"He does."

"Grandison?"

"Yes, that's her will. Of course, they keep hoping Mathilda's still alive. They can't do anything about the money yet."

"Meanwhile, he still controls it?"

"Of course."

Francis thought awhile. "How can I get to Althea?"

"What do you mean, get to her?"

"Talk to her. Get to know her. Well enough to ask a lot of interesting questions."

"You can't," said Jane. "There's no way." He looked at her. "Listen, Fran; in the first place, she's a bride. She and Oliver are still honeymooning. She sticks around their crowd, besides, and it's a closed crowd. Nobody could get in."

"Want to bet?"

"No, because I know. Grandy'd never bother with somebody just nice and ordinary and civilized and in between, like you, Fran. Somebody famous, maybe. Or somebody very humble. But not you. And, you see, if he didn't take you up, you'd never get to Althea."

"Is that so?" said Francis with a kind of mild surprise. "Could I get in there as a servant? I've never tried, but I don't doubt I could be a butler, for instance."

"No servants."

"No servants at all!"

"Not a one. He doesn't believe in them. He says they'd limit his complete freedom."

"No chauffeur, even?"

"Oh, no. He drives himself around in an old jalopy. He wears an old brown hat."

"I could be the gas man."

"Where would that get you?"

"Nowhere," he admitted. He drummed his fingers on the table.

"Fran," she said, "remember, I'm in there, after all."

"You lie low, Auntie Jane." He smiled. The absurdity of their relationship amused him once more. His father's baby sister, Jane was. His cute little Aunt Jane. "You keep your little old nose out of this. In fact, maybe you'd better not go back at all."

"Oh, don't worry. He thinks I'm a dumb blonde."

"Lots of people do, and they're so wrong," said Francis. "How am I going to get in there? Couldn't I pretend to be some famous character?"

"I doubt if you could hoax him. He's such a shrewd old—"

"Never mind. Would it be possible for you to lure Althea out to meet me?"

"Althea thinks the sun rises and sets with her Grandy," Jane warned him.

"How about this Oliver? What kind of guy is he?"

Jane wrinkled her nose. "Oh, he's all right. He's pleasant. He's the kind of man who understands women's hats."

"Lord."

"Of course, he thinks Grandy's practically God. They all do."

"Maybe Grandy does," said Francis grimly.

They both drank some coffee. He tried again. "Could I hire myself out to that lawyer, get into his office?"

"I don't know, Fran, I don't think you'd find anything. Surely he wouldn't let there be records."

Francis shook his head. "How did Rosaleen find out?"

Jane looked blank.

"Instinct tells me I've got to get to know Althea," he insisted.

"But, Fran, how could I lure her out? What could I say? 'Come and meet somebody who thinks your guardian is a stinker'? And if you hinted anything like that, she'd go straight back to Grandy—"

"Then you mustn't have anything to do with my meeting her," said Francis promptly. "I see. And yet I've got to get at her."

"You watch out for Althea. She's got silver eyes."

"Do you think," said Francis, and suddenly he looked very old, "that any woman, with or without silver eyes, is going to bother me?"

Jane drank some more coffee. Francis was looking down. She hated the drawn line of his cheek, the too-thin look of him. This wasn't the Francis she loved, who was sure of things, the one all other girls immediately assumed to be mysterious and exciting. He wasn't mysterious to her, not even now. She was his little old Aunt

Jane, and she knew what ailed him was only sorrow, and that bitter anger he was holding leashed and ready. And God knew what he'd been through in the war, besides.

But Fran, bitter and old, missing that something wild and nimble in his spirit, that quicksilver quality. She thought, outraged, *He's only twenty-five.* She babbled out loud, unhappily, "I'm not belittling your fatal charm, darling. But it's not a good moment to establish yourself as Althea's boy friend."

"Let it go," said Francis irritably. Then, in a minute, he lifted his head. "Suppose I were Mathilda's boy friend?"

Jane felt a little shock. "They say— I mean, there wasn't anyone but Oliver."

"They're so wrong," said Francis softly. He kept his head up. She saw his nostrils quiver. "How old was Mathilda?"

"Twenty-two."

"That's fine. I think I'll be Mathilda's boy friend, all upset because she's drowned."

"But Fran—"

"When did she sail on this fatal ship?"

"In January."

"From New York? Alone?"

"Uh-huh."

"Then she met me in New York. I'm a new boy friend."

"But, Fran, she went off with a broken heart. You can't pretend—"

He wasn't listening. He went ahead. "Was she here in the city long before she sailed? How long, Jane?"

"Three days."

"All that time?" said Francis, in a pleased way. "And she was alone?"

"She was alone. Don't you see, it must have been that she ran away from the situation. There was that newly married pair moving in. Althea'd copped off her man. It must have been a hideous blow."

He didn't say anything. Jane, watching him, suddenly remembered the time he'd gone out and bet his allowance on a horse race, and won enough to buy his mother a wildly extravagant bracelet for Christmas. He had just that crazy gleam, that funny high-sailing look, as if now he wasn't going to bother to use the ground. He was going to take to the air. His spurning look. He'd get these reckless streaks, as if something in his will, or something mysteriously lucky, or some fantastic kind of foresight, would signal to him. He'd scare everybody to death. Then it would come out all right. This was the old Fran, the one she loved, with that leaping look.

"By gum, why didn't I marry the girl?" he asked, as if this were a reasonable question.

Her heart turned over. "Marry what girl?"

"Mathilda. Obviously, I married Mathilda."

"No! Fran!"

"Now, wait. Think about it. Be logical."

"Logical!" said Jane. "Oh, gosh! Logical!" She hung on to the table. "Now, just a min—"

"But that does it! She's the one with the money. See here, Jane, sooner or later won't they have to presume she's not coming back from her watery grave? Ah-ha, but when she married me, you know, she technically got control of her own money. So I'm the guy that'll be right there, asking bright, intelligent questions, when the books are opened."

Jane stuttered, "She w-willed it to Grandy."

"Never mind." He brushed her off. "I'll fix that. I'm an interested party. That's enough. That'll do it. And besides—look, honey. I go up there. Most natural thing in the world. My God, my bride! I'm all upset. I want to be with her nearest and dearest. Don't I? So I talk about her. So I talk. I talk to everybody. I talk to Althea.

I'm a tragic figure. Althea's going to be powerful sorry for me." His eyebrows flew up. He looked full of the devil.

"But, Fran—"

"Don't say 'But, Fran.' Ask questions. Be helpful."

"No, no. Listen." Jane struck the table with her fist. "Don't underrate that man! Don't dare! Please don't try anything half-baked. He's too smart, too terribly smart! This isn't any parlor game. You can't just go and tell a plain lie and expect him to swallow it. You said it yourself. Assume he's guilty. Then he's bound to check. He'll be very wary."

"Let him check," said Francis coldly. "Let him be wary."

Jane closed her eyes. She heard his voice go on, now quick and excited.

"What you do is, you go back. Send me her handwriting. All you can find. Steal it. Send me pictures of her. Good ones."

"But, Fran—"

"Got to have them. Think about it."

"There's a roll," said Jane slowly, as if he had hypnotized her, "that Althea had in her camera. She had them developed last week and they all cried over the ones with Mathilda."

"Those are the ones I want."

"But, Fran—"

"Don't 'but.'"

"Fran, you're crazy!" She opened her eyes.

"Am I?" said Francis quietly. "O.K. The point is, I intend to get in there and find out what happened to Rosaleen. Because if anybody hurt her, he will get hurt. I don't mind what methods I use, or what trouble I take, or what lies I tell, or bribes I have to pay. If this is the way you get in and find out, then this is the way I go. You can't stop me. I don't think you want to, really. You might as well help, don't you think?"

"I'd h-help," she stammered. "But, Fran, Mathilda could not have—"

"You don't understand her psychology," he said whimsically.

"But, Fran!"

"But what?"

"But everything!" she wailed.

Francis leaned back. He was smiling. She thought, *He's lost ten years*. He looked like a man who contemplated moving heaven and earth with bright, interested eyes. "Ask me something I can't answer," he challenged, "so I can fix up some answers."

3

The April morning was sunny, cool and clear. Down in her stateroom, the girl with the green eyes took a last look at herself in the mirror door. Her old tweed suit was, she thought, respectable enough. She was lucky to have found it, forgotten in the Bermuda clothes closet. The black shoes weren't quite right, but they would have to do. She had no hat. The scarf she'd knotted around her head like a turban had blown away one day on deck. She wore her gold-brown hair very plain. It was clean and shining. For the first time in her life, she hadn't felt able to spend the money to have her hair done, so she had washed it herself, carefully. A good job, she thought. No gloves. Just this old brown-and-white summer bag. She picked it up.

Her luggage had already gone, such as it was. One nightgown, one toothbrush and a bag of very expensive Dutch chocolates rattling lonesomely in the clumsy suitcase. She'd spent half of what she had left for the chocolates; each one of them was just about worth its weight in gold. Well, but he loved them so. He must have them. It would make him so happy.

She smiled, and saw herself smile in the glass. Yes, she thought, she must remember to smile. Her face had grown thinner. It was bonier than ever now. Better smile. It wouldn't do to look woebegone or exhausted. She wasn't really, except for reasons that had nothing to do with what they would want to know. Not that they wouldn't love to know the real reasons.

She turned for a last look at her stocking seams. She felt very calm. She knew exactly how to behave. She opened the door of her stateroom and walked down the corridor.

An officer spoke to her. "They're waiting for you."

"Thank you."

Be a lady. Smile. Be pleasant. Be sweet and dull. She remembered her lessons.

The officer took her into the room where they were—several men and one girl. Their eyes licked at her.

The officer said, "This is Miss Mathilda Frazier."

She said quietly and in a friendly fashion, "How do you do?"

The cameras popped off like a quick lightning storm. They flashed one after another. Mathilda stood still, her lips curved pleasantly and a little shyly.

Grandy'd told her long ago, "Tyl, you're an heiress and, for various reasons deeply ingrained in the fundamentals of human nature, my dear, that fact makes what you do several times as interesting as what other girls do. Now, Althea, being penniless, doesn't have quite the same problem. Yet Althea, with her great beauty, has her own trouble."

She shook off the memory of Grandy, sitting in his favorite chair. Never mind Althea now. The point was, he'd taught her how to handle this. Dear Grandy, he'd taught her so much. Her heart felt warm when she thought of him.

The men of the press took an impression that she was well-bred, that she was shy. One or two of them approved of her ankles. It was the female among them who realized that, although her clothes were dull, this girl was beautifully made and essentially lovely. One of them suggested that she might like to tell her story in her own way.

"Never give them an emotion," Grandy used to say. "Look placid, dear. Placid as a milkmaid. That's the way."

"I was reading in my room when the ship caught fire," she began. "There was an alarm, of course. I took my coat and went up to my boat station. They lowered the boat almost immediately. It was all very orderly."

She stopped and smiled the shy little smile. But it was too brief, too bare. They began to question.

"Were you hurt, Miss Frazier?" someone said warmly.

"No, not at all."

"Did you see the fire?"

"No," she said. "I couldn't see anything."

"No smoke? No flames?"

"It must have been at the other side of the ship," she said in her clear, gentle voice.

"Were the passengers scared? Any panic?"

"Not that I saw," she answered. Better leave out about Doctor Phillips, praying so loud, arguing with the Lord under the stars. And how surprised he was when his prayer was so promptly and practically answered. He'd even, she remembered, seemed a little disappointed and thwarted, as if he'd had a lot of prayer in him yet, O Lord. "We were picked up in only two hours," she said.

"Who was in your lifeboat?"

"There were twelve of us passengers, and three crew members."

"Was it cold? Was the weather bad? Did you suffer?"

"It was quite warm," said Mathilda. "It was a lovely night."

One of the newsmen was a little redheaded fellow, a fidgeter. "O.K., so you got picked up."

"The S.S. *Blayne*," said one of them. Somebody sighed impatiently.

"How come they took you all the way to Africa?"

"I don't know," said Mathilda. *Never guess when you don't know.*

"Did you realize that no message came through from you?"

"We couldn't be sure," she said a little too quickly. *Be careful. Don't say too much.* She went on more slowly, with a little frown, as if she were taking pains. "Of course we tried. But they wouldn't use the ship's radio. And the port where we were taken was quite confused."

She looked straight at the female one. They would have no way to guess how she'd felt about it, how she hadn't really made much of an effort to get a message through. Mathilda knew now that it had been childish, that mood of not trying, that babyish, rebellious thought. *Let him think I died. Then he'll be sorry.* Her heart bounced, as it always did with the thought of Oliver or even at a hint that she was about to think of him. *Push it down.*

"What happened there?" somebody was asking.

"At the African port, you mean? Why, just waiting, really. You see, although we had to wait so long for a returning ship, we never knew but what we might be sailing the next morning. So we were busy waiting." *Watch it. Don't be colorful.*

"Where did you stay?"

"At a very nice little hotel." She saw it vividly—more vividly, almost, than she could see anything else in her memory. It was brilliant in the sun, that terrible aching sunlight that had poured over everything. And she could smell it. But she mustn't say so. Nor must she give them any hint of the brooding pain that filled all her days there under that brutal sun, the headache and the heartache all mingled together.

"But what did you do with yourselves?"

"Do?" she repeated slowly. *Take your time.*

"Yes, while you waited."

"We tried to be patient," she said gently. "Sometimes we played cards. There wasn't much to read."

Their faces were getting bleaker and bleaker. She knew they wanted adventure. And yet, she thought, honestly there hadn't been anything adventurous. Or if there had, she hadn't recognized it. Maybe someday, when she was old and looked back, details such as flies and headaches would have faded out; maybe it would look like an adventure then.

"Weren't there any interesting people?" asked the one who was a girl.

"Very nice people," said Mathilda primly. "There was Doctor Phillips and his wife. He is a clergyman. There were Mr. and Mrs. Stevens—"

"No men?"

"Oh, yes."

"Young men?"

"N-no," said Mathilda. "At least not younger than about forty." Mr. Boyleston had been forty. He had only one eye, but better not say so.

"No natives?"

"Of course there were natives," said Mathilda. "Although we didn't see very much of them."

Something eager was dying out of their faces. They were giving her up. All except the red-haired man, who still watched her face as if he were searching for signs.

"But finally you got a ship, huh?"

"Yes, finally we did," she said brightly. "It took us to Buenos Aires."

"That message gave the whole country a thrill. In fact, you made Page One."

Mathilda smiled politely and moistened her lips. *Was it thrill-*

ing to Oliver? she wondered with the familiar sickening lurch of her heart.

"There was a chance to fly to Bermuda, and I took it," she said, "because I have a house there and people knew me." She glanced down at her suit. Better not go into the ragged crew they'd been.

"Did you have any money, Miss Frazier?"

"People were very kind," she said evasively. She kept smiling. *Don't boast.* Better not let them know that the mere rumor of her wealth had inspired enough kindness to bring them home.

"What do you plan to do now?"

"I must get home," she said. Was Oliver there? Was Althea there? Mustn't ask.

"To Dedham, you mean, of course? To Mr. Grandison's house? He broadcast a piece about you," said the female one chattily. "'Tyl, dear, wherever you may be—' He had me bawling."

Mathilda's eyes stung. *Don't give them an emotion, even a good one.* She swallowed.

"I'll bet you're glad to be back," said the red-haired man, not perfunctorily, but as if he alone knew why.

"Yes, I am. Very glad indeed." Her green eyes met his steadily. *You can end any interview after a decent passage of time.*

"It must have been quite an adventure," said the female one a little flatly, as if she doubted it.

"Yes," said Mathilda. "I really think that's about all I can tell you. If you'll excuse me. Thank you for being so kind." *Always thank them.*

"Well, thank you." "Thanks a lot." They were through with her. They made as if to withdraw, all but the red-haired man, who drew closer.

"Why are you using your maiden name?" he said in a low, conversational tone.

Mathilda caught hold of her surprise and alarm and controlled it. Just her lashes flickered. "I beg your pardon?" she murmured. She took a step away. She was afraid, if he got too close, the emotional tension she was hiding so carefully would be palpable, like a magnetic field.

"He's waiting for you on the pier," said the red-haired man.

"Who?" She hadn't meant to ask. *Mustn't get involved.* This was the press. *Never converse. Recite.*

"Your husband," said the red-haired man.

Mathilda didn't move, didn't say anything. It took all her training to stand so still. The thought of Oliver broke through and flooded her whole mind. Could it be Oliver who was waiting at the pier? By some miracle, restored to her? As if Althea had never so easily, so almost lazily, reached out and taken him away? Her heart pounded.

"All I'm asking is: Do you confirm it or deny?" said the red-haired man in a rapid mutter. "How about it, Mrs. Howard? Can I take that blush—"

Mathilda said, "If you'll excuse me, please." She looked full at him, although she couldn't see his face. She could feel her lips mechanically smiling.

"What goes on?" said the female one, abruptly popping up beside them.

The red-haired man was sending Mathilda a hurt, reproachful look, but she didn't see it. She said again, still smiling, "Won't you please excuse me now?"

"O.K.," said the red-haired man. "O.K." But he said it as if he were saying, "All right for you."

Mathilda went and sat quietly in a corner of the deck. "Such a nice, quiet girl," Mrs. Stevens had told the reporters. "Such a little lady. Why not the least bit conscious of all that money. We have become very close friends," said Mrs. Stevens, with plenty of consciousness of all that money.

So the Stevenses came and fluttered around her, all talking at once, promising to look her up, never to forget her, begging her to promise them the same. Mathilda kept promising.

But the whole thing was back now in full force. Just as strong as if she'd never been shipwrecked and carried away to Africa, half the world away. She could see, bitterly, Oliver's face as it had been two days before their wedding day, when he had come in and been so strangely silent. She had babbled innocently along, happily, naively, all unwarned, unprepared, about who had sent what present, about such silly little things. And at last, when she'd stopped the chatter, puzzled, he'd said, "Tyl, are you happy?" And she'd been so startled. The whole thing had caught her in the throat. She'd finally answered in the extravagant language she never naturally used, simply because it meant too much; she couldn't answer him otherwise. She'd turned her back and cried, "Darling, of course, I'm just about out of my mind with happiness! Aren't you?"

He'd said, "Well, don't worry," in that flat blunt voice that wasn't like Oliver at all. And when, in surprise, she'd turned around, he'd been gone. Gone.

Nor had she, even then, understood anything. How dumb! How could she have been so dumb? Stupid. Blind. Dumb. Did she crack wise? Oh, no, not she! Not dumb-bunny Mathilda, the ugly duckling with all the money.

Grandy'd had to take her aside into his study that night, with only one dim light, she remembered. Sitting beside her in the shadows, he'd told her in his gentlest voice, "Tyl, darling, I think this belated honesty of Oliver's is lucky for you. Oh, I realize that you won't see beyond the surface humiliation and it's true. Oliver ought to have told you more directly. Poor duckling. But this superficial blow to your pride is nothing, nothing. You must believe me. Someday you will know that this is right. Someday you will know that Oliver, however clumsily he's done it, hasn't really done you wrong."

Maybe. Maybe. Maybe. But Oliver was lost and there was a whole structure of dream and plan that tumbled down. And she had to learn all over again to be alone. And why did it have to be Althea? Damn her. Oh, damn her.

All her remembered life, Althea had been there with that power to take away. Never had Tyl had a glow, a hint of success, of happiness, that Althea hadn't somehow been able to dim it or put it out. Poor penniless Althea, who was so beautiful. Tyl ground her teeth.

"Nor must you blame Althea," Grandy'd said. "You must be charitable, my dear. She was in love."

"I know," she'd answered with a proud tolerance, biting back the cry, *But so was I! But so was I!* And still, in April, her heart was crying, *But so was I!*

"Won't it be wonderful to see all our friends?" sighed Mrs. Stevens. "Just think; any minute. Won't you come around to the other side, Miss Frazier, dear?"

Mathilda said desperately, "Won't you please excuse me?"

4

Mathilda's luggage didn't keep her long. She seemed hardly to have begun to remember how to stand up on land, when they were finished with her. She was through customs, standing in another lightning storm of cameras, and a tall man had come up to her with a protective air.

Blinded, Mathilda couldn't quite see his face, but she heard a strange, kind voice saying close to her ear, "Grandy let me come." Her eyes filled with tears of relief. She felt a gush of emotion, a sense of coming home.

The red-haired newsman saw her falter and begin to cry; saw the tall man, with a kind swoop of his whole body that seemed to surround her and guard her, guide her quickly through the groups of people and put her into a cab, very neatly, very fast. The red-haired man ran his tongue around an upper molar. He might have been sneering.

Mathilda stumbled into the taxi. It took her a minute to find a handkerchief. The man beside her, with an odd effect of pure and scientific curiosity, said, "Why is it they call Althea the beautiful one?"

"Because she is, of course," said Mathilda in honest surprise. Now she could see his face. It wasn't a face she had ever seen before. He was dark—dark hair, weathered skin. His eyes were dark, with heavy lashes. He had the kind of nose that suggests good humor, a nose not in the least chiseled or sharp, but boyish looking. His chin was firm. His face was thin, with no puffs of flesh. It was a formed face, the face of a man who had been, somehow, tested, although he was young. His eyebrows went up at an angle toward his temples. There was something gay about the way they flew when he smiled.

He spoke again before she had time to form a question. "Grandy would have come down. He wanted to. But he thought it would only complicate the publicity part."

Into her mind flitted the memory of the red-haired man and what he'd said. But the thought flitted out again. "Where are we going?"

"To a hotel. I have to pick up my stuff. And I want very much to talk to you."

He did have a nice smile. But it came over Mathilda, just the same, that all this was rather strange. Grandy's mere name had been enough for that moment on the pier. But now she drew a little away, shrinking back into her own corner of the taxicab.

"I want to talk to you quite seriously," he was continuing. She began to feel alarmed. He said lightly, "I'm afraid your Mr. Grandison has been up to some plain and fancy dirty work."

Mathilda took a deep breath. Her green eyes opened wider.

The man said, "I don't know where to start. I suppose it began with Jane—but of course you don't know Jane."

"I don't know you," said Mathilda coldly. "Will you please ask the man to take us to the station? I would like to go to Mr. Grandison's house by the first train."

He looked as if he hadn't quite taken in what she said. He sat still. If he'd been in a movie, you'd have assumed that the film had stuck. His eyes remained interested and alert. He made no move to redirect the cab driver.

"I haven't the faintest idea who you are," said Mathilda angrily, "and you may as well know that I will not listen to your opinions of Mr. Grandison. Since I've never seen you before in my life, I am perfectly sure you can't know Mr. Grandison anything like as well as I do. And you ought to know better than to think you can run him down to me."

He said nothing. Something about his pose collapsed just a little, as if a little air had gone out of a balloon. There was a small crumpling.

Mathilda was mad as hops. This was no newsman. She could let fly. She could be as vivid and as colorful with her emotion as she liked. She said, "Grandy has taken care of me since I was nine. He's been my father and my mother and my uncles and my aunts. He's taught me all I know and given me just about everything I've ever had of any value. All the things you can't buy. He's given me my home. He made it home for me. He's picked my schools. He's cared. He's spent thought and trouble on me. He's my family. And not because we have the same blood, either, but because he wanted to be, because he loved me and I love him. He is, in my considered opinion, the best and wisest man in the world, and anything he chooses to do is all right with me, and always will be. And if you won't tell the cab driver where to go, I will. Or I'll scream. Choose one!"

She saw, through her anger, with satisfaction that the man had really collapsed now. At least he had fallen back into his corner and was sitting there somberly, and it was as if he were locked inside a shell of very thick silence. He was saying nothing in seventeen different languages. He was stopped, gagged. He'd shut his mouth. *Well*, she thought, *he'd better*.

"Driver," said Mathilda.

The man got some words out painfully. "No, don't," he said. "We are to telephone."

"There are telephones everywhere," she said coldly. "Particularly in the Grand Central Station."

"Yes, but my—" He pulled himself together in order to speak at all. "Grandy sent me," he said. "Nobody's going to hurt you, you know. You don't really think so, do you?"

"Certainly not," said Mathilda with airy contempt.

"No train for an hour and a half," he said. He seemed rather indifferent suddenly. He looked out of the cab window, away from her. "If you like, I'll leave you after we telephone. You'll have to wait somewhere."

Mathilda sat back. She was still seething. She tried to remember exactly what he had said that had set off so much anger. But the phrase didn't come back to her accurately. She began to feel that she'd been too vehement. She had made a show of herself. She understood, now, that it had all been part of the home-coming emotion somehow.

His withdrawn silence smacked of reproach. After all, if Grandy had sent him— She cast about for some remark, something in the way of small talk, to indicate that the storm was over. She said chattily, "I hope you realize that I don't even know your name."

He did a strange thing. He put his hand up and covered his eyes, and sat very still and tense. She wondered if he had heard. "I don't know your name," she repeated.

"My name is Francis Howard," he said stiffly. He took his hand down and went back to looking out of the cab window. She could see his ear, the line of his cheek, not his eyes.

Howard. Mathilda's mind took what she at first thought was a capricious swoop, back to the interview with the press. Then she cried out, "Howard!"

He didn't look around, though he moved his head a trifle warily.

"That was funny!" Mathilda said. "There was one man who seemed to think— He said my husband— Why, that's what he called me! Mrs. Howard!"

"He did?" said Mr. Howard, in a bored, perfunctory way.

And he said no more. Mathilda stopped talking. Really, he was the limit. Certainly it was an odd thing to have been said and the coincidence was very odd. "Your husband is waiting for you, Mrs. Howard." Any normal human being, thought Mathilda indignantly, would want to know all about it, especially when it was the same name. He wouldn't just sit, looking indifferently away, out of the window.

The cab pulled up. A doorman helped them out, a bellhop came for her suitcase. She knew the place. Francis guided her into the lobby, into the elevator. Mathilda stood stiff and cold. The funny thing was that just as they walked into the elevator, as he gave the floor number to the boy, she caught a flash of his eye on her, and it was a look of both impatience and anger. Mathilda bit hard on her teeth. He had no business being angry with her, for the love of Mike! She marched down the corridor after the bellboy, holding her head haughtily.

They were admitted to a suite. Mathilda stood in the middle of the floor. She indicated the telephone. Francis was muttering to the bellboy about trains, bags. Without a word to her, he crossed to the telephone and asked for Grandy's number. He sat hunched over the phone, his right arm dangling. The call went through without much delay.

"Hello. . . . Jane?"

Mathilda thought, *Now, who is Jane*? It seemed to her that he'd mentioned a Jane before.

"Francis," said Francis. . . . "Yes, she's here." He looked around at Mathilda coldly, as if to say, "What, are you listening to a private conversation?" He said, as if he were speaking in code, "Is everybody well?" Then he said, with a hint of desperation, "Jane, can you get out? And I mean now?"

"Why, no," said Jane cheerfully from Connecticut, "of course not. He's right here, Mr. Howard. Here he is!"

Grandy's voice took her place. "My dear boy, is she really with you?"

"She's here," he said again, this time with a very odd inflection. He held out the phone to Mathilda. She took it, surprised, touched, excited, and suddenly ready to weep again.

"Oh, Grandy, darling!"

"Mathilda, little duck, are you all right? You're back? You're safe?"

"I'm fine," she quavered. "Oh, Grandy, I want to see you."

"Don't cry," said Grandy. "Don't cry. God bless us every one. What a darling you are to telephone. Are you happy?"

"Oh, Grandy!"

"Tell Francis to bring you home."

"I will, I will. I'm coming just as fast—"

"Strawberries and cream, Tyl," said Grandy. "You hurry, sweetheart."

He hung up and she hung up, sobbing. Strawberries and cream was her special treat. How like him! How dear!

Mr. Howard was standing with his hands in his pockets, staring out the window.

"Grandy says you're to bring me home." She was willing to smile at him now.

He turned around. She thought, with a shock, *Something's hurt him. He's going to cry.*

He said in a low, vibrant voice that startled her with its passionate appeal, "Tyl, don't you remember?"

5

"Remember what?"

He started to pull his hands out of his pockets and then thrust them deeper instead. "Never mind. Foolish question. Obviously, you don't. You can't or you—" He came one step nearer. "Tyl, what happened to you? Were you hurt, darling? You must have been . . . ill for part of the time. That's so, isn't it?" Everything in his manner begged her to say yes.

"No," said Mathilda. "That isn't so."

"But it must be so, and you've forgotten that too."

"I haven't forgotten anything!" she cried. "I wish you'd tell me! Who are you and what am I supposed to—"

"I'm your husband," he said sharply, almost angrily.

She backed away a little. In her mind was a vague idea of mistaken identity. "Are you sure you know who I am?" she asked gently. "My name is Mathilda Frazier. I have no husband. I'm not married."

He moved away from her, and with his hands still in his pockets, almost as if he didn't dare to take them out, he sat down on a straight chair, keeping his feet close together. He looked like a man controlling himself at some cost.

"Sorry," he said. "Let's try to straighten this out, shall we?"

He smiled. Mathilda moved to another chair and sat down in it. Her knees felt a little shaky. It was just as well to sit down.

"Yes, please," she agreed.

They sat looking at each other.

"Do you remember," said Francis finally, in a quiet conversational tone, "when you left Grandy's house, that Sunday afternoon last January, to come to New York?"

Mathilda nodded. She thought, *But he knows Grandy. It can't be that he's mistaken me for someone else.*

"You came to this hotel," he was saying. "Do you remember that?"

"Yes," said Mathilda. "Yes, of course I did. Not this room."

"You were in Seven-o-five," he stated. The number seemed right to her. She could not have recollected it, but she recognized it. "You had some supper sent up," he went on. She nodded. "But a little later, about nine o'clock, you went down to the lobby."

"No," said Mathilda bluntly. Not at all. It was not so. She had crawled into bed to read. She hadn't been able to read or sleep either. She remembered getting up to look for aspirin, waiting for drowsiness that would not come, the desperate tricks she had tried to play on her own mind, the getting up at last to sit by the window, holding her head.

"So that's where it begins," the man was saying.

"Where what begins?"

"Your forgetting."

"But I— What is it you say I've forgotten?"

"You came downstairs about nine o'clock," he told her, "that Sunday evening. You were pretty distressed; you were feeling pretty sick about Oliver."

A thrill of dismay and excitement went through Mathilda. How did he know that?

"So you were restless and you came down to get something to

read. It was a kind of excuse to get away from your room. You hated to go back. You drifted across the lobby toward the grillroom. That's when I saw you."

Mathilda said, "You couldn't have seen me. I didn't leave my room that Sunday night."

"Please," he begged. He closed his eyes. "You made me think of flying," he said in quite a different voice. "You made me think of the sky or a bird. You're like a Winged Victory in modern dress, but with better ankles. You've got such a tearing beauty, Tyl—you're windblown. It's in your bones, your long, lovely legs, the way you walk, your face, your nose. The molding of the upper part of your cheek, around the outside of your eye. I've dreamed about it. And how that dear old soul, your Luther Grandison, can be so blind as to call you his ugly duckling and never see the swan! Why, Tyl, don't you know you make Althea look like a lump of paste?"

Mathilda heard what he said; she heard the words. But her mind went spinning off into confusion. How could he say such things? How could such things be said at all? She tightened her fingers around her purse. She felt a little dizzy. She was used to people saying kind words about her looks. It was because she was so rich. She told herself that this, too, must be deliberate flattery, because she was so rich.

He opened his eyes, he smiled. His voice sank back as if it had begun to tire. "Maybe I'd better make it plain right away. I fell in love with you, Mathilda, but you didn't fall in love with me. I knew that. I still know it. If you only had, maybe you wouldn't have forgotten."

Mathilda took hold of herself. She dismissed the thought that someone must have gone mad. It wasn't helpful. She must think better than that. "Why are you trying to make me believe something I know is not so?" she asked quietly. "I do know, because I remember every minute of that time. There is nothing I've forgotten. I haven't been hurt or sick. I know exactly what happened to me in this hotel while I was here, and everything that has happened since. There is no gap." She straightened her shoulders. "I thought at first you might be honestly mistaken. You'd somehow or other got me mixed up with some other girl. But now I see you aren't mistaken, Mr. Howard. You're just lying. I'd like to know why."

He shut his eyes to hide a brief gleam that baffled her. He groaned. He took his hands out of his pockets and held his head for a moment. Then his hands fell, relaxed and open, and he said, "My poor Tyl. Don't—don't be upset."

But Mathilda was thinking hard. "What about Grandy?" she cried. "Grandy knows you! Does Grandy think—"

"Yes," he said, "I've been—well, I've been staying there."

Mathilda got up. She was furious. "So that's why, is it? You've wormed your way into Grandy's house! Are you trying to cheat him, some way? What was it you said? Something about dirty work? What are you trying to do to Grandy?"

"My dear—"

"Using my name! Using me!" she stormed. "You probably thought I was dead. Didn't you?"

"Perhaps I did," he murmured. He was sitting still, watching her anger almost as if it couldn't hurt him personally, but he was curious about it, examining it, studying it.

"You'd better tell me right away what you meant in the taxicab. About Grandy."

"I was being facetious," he said in a monotone.

"Oh, nonsense! Who's Jane?"

"Jane is Grandy's secretary."

"Where's Rosaleen?"

"Why, she's . . . not there any more," he said. "If you'll try to listen, I'll tell you what I meant in the taxicab." And she caught again that faint hint of antagonism as he looked up at her.

"If you please," said Mathilda grandly in her coldest voice, and she sat down stiffly.

"I was simply making small talk," said Francis. "I was going on to tell you how Grandy hijacked those strawberries."

"I don't believe you. Why did you all of a sudden act so collapsed? You crawled into the corner—"

"What you said," he murmured wearily.

"What?"

He made an effort. "You said, 'I don't know you.'" Mathilda was silent. "If you will try to accept this weird business that you and I remember the same period of time, the same place, entirely differently. If you will just for one brief second imagine me sitting there, with my wife, my lost girl, found again. Trying like the very devil not to break down and bawl. Thinking in my innocence that you understood, that we were putting off the real—greeting, shall I say?—until we could be alone. And then, without any warning whatsoever, you say—what you said. 'I don't know you. I haven't the faintest idea who you are.'"

Mathilda swallowed hard. "Have you been hurt or ill lately, Mr. Howard?"

He got up and went back to looking out the window with his back to her.

Mathilda said with malice, "My father left me a great deal of money."

He swung around. She controlled an impulse to cringe. But he was smiling. "Why, so did mine," he said pleasantly. "I'm nearly as rich as you are, sweetie pie." Astonishment crossed her face and he laughed. Then he came nearer and spoke very gently. "It was just love," he said. "I'm sorry you don't remember."

The bell rang. It was the porter, come to get the bags. He touched his cap. "How do, Mrs. Howard."

Shock sent Mathilda out of her chair. She crowded back against the desk. She was frightened now.

"Just a minute," said Francis. "Jimmy, will you do us a favor? Just tell Mrs. Howard when you last saw her."

"Why, lemme see, back in January. Last I saw her was Wednesday morning, right after the wedding. You gave me—"

"But I'm not married!"

The man looked distressed. "Honest, I never said anything. I never— I'd like to say I'm glad you got back safe, Mrs. Howard," the man stammered.

Mathilda turned away. Behind her, she knew Francis was giving him money. She heard him say, "Forget about this, Jimmy. Mrs. Howard's been ill."

She clenched her fists. So that would be his story. And she couldn't make a scene here, in front of a hotel servant. Or anywhere. She couldn't run to strangers or cry out that he lied. Not Mathilda Frazier. Not the long-lost heiress. No, never.

She must get home. Get to Grandy, who would know what to do. Just hold on to what she knew to be so, remember that he was lying, trying for some unknown reason to—to do what? Never mind now. Keep controlled. Get to Grandy as soon as she could.

But, she thought, it's not the truth. That porter is lying too.

She said, quite calmly, when the man had gone, "He was bribed."

Francis made no answer. She said, with more anger than she wished to show, "I dare say you forged a marriage certificate. Why don't you show me that?"

"Because the bride keeps the marriage certificate," he said slowly, "and I imagine you . . . lost it."

"No papers?" she sneered.

"Some," he said. "Look here, Tyl. Don't—don't hate me. Don't. I'm not trying— Please, can't we try to be a little bit friendly about this?"

He really did look upset and distressed, but she said coldly, "I think we'd better go to the station."

"Very well," he said.

She started toward the door. She stopped. "What papers?" she demanded. He shook his head. "I want to know how you managed to deceive Grandy!" she cried.

His face went black with emotion, suddenly. "Look here," he said roughly, "you hurt. You don't seem to know it, but I'll be damned if I see why I have to . . . be hurt. Either you listen to my entire story, let me tell you the whole thing, all that happened, all you've forgotten—which seems to me the fair thing for you to do, by the way—or we'll say no more about it I'll see you to the train. And good-by. You can divorce me, get an annulment, do whatever you like. Ignore the whole thing. I'm not likely," he stated bitterly, "to want to marry anyone else for a while."

Mathilda hesitated. She thought, *I don't understand*. Her mind rebelled at its own confusion. It seemed to her that this man had been forcing her into confusion, and she wanted to fight back. She wanted to feel clear, to understand better. It was a way of fighting. She went back and sat down in her chair.

"Very well. Tell me," she said.

6

"YOU WERE, as I said, standing near the grillroom. I saw you. I made up my mind to have a try at picking you up." He was speaking bitterly, bluntly and fast. "It worked. You were lonely and upset. You needed to talk to someone. We went into a corner of the bar and you did talk. You told me all about Oliver and Althea and what had happened to you. You were hurt, then; so hurt, my dear, so heartsore." His voice warmed, "I don't suppose you realized at all what was happening to me. I don't suppose you really saw me that Sunday night.

"I was someone to listen. A stranger, who wouldn't care, you thought, who wouldn't tell. Who'd listen and be sympathetic, and go away taking some of your trouble with him just by virtue of having listened. It didn't work out that way, because I fell in love, and I am a very persistent fellow and I would not go away. I'm afraid I hung around. We were together Monday. Had lunch. Roamed around. In the evening, we went back to our corner in the bar. This time, I talked. I told you I was in the Air Force, but I was being let out. I told you quite a bit. You listened. I wonder if you heard."

Mathilda closed her eyes, squeezed them tight. But when she opened them, he was still there, still talking.

"Tuesday," he said, "well, on Tuesday, in the morning, you said you'd marry me."

"Why?"

He took her up quickly. "Why you said you'd marry me, I . . . don't know. You never said you felt anything for me but just . . . comfortable in my presence. It was one of those half-cold-blooded things. I knew I was getting you on a rebound. And, Tyl, darling, I knew perfectly well that there was a little bit of a nasty human wish for revenge in your heart."

She frowned, but her heart had jumped in surprise.

"Oh, yes, that was obvious." he went on. "But I was going to get you on any terms at all. So I was pretty unscrupulous. Who am I to take a high moral tone? And you—honey, it was babyish, but I understood, still understand. It wasn't so much revenge on Oliver, the poor sap, but on Althea, the louse." He grinned.

"I—I see," said Mathilda dazedly. He leaned forward. His eyes searched her face. "No, no," she said. "No, I don't mean that I remember. It just sounds— It didn't happen, but you make it sound as if— I can see it might have."

He said, with an unfathomable expression in his dark eyes, "Thank you, Tyl." He went on, "At ten in the morning, Wednesday, we were married."

"It can't be done!" she gasped.

"It was done," he said calmly. "Are you thinking of all the red tape? It wasn't so bad. You already had your blood test. You had been all set to marry somebody else."

She winced.

"I had only to get a certificate from the medical officer. And they waive the waiting period, you know, for men in the service." He took something out of his pocket "We got the license Tuesday. I do have a copy."

Tyl looked and saw "WHITE PLAINS, NEW YORK. MARY FRAZIER. JOHN FRANCIS HOWARD."

"That's not my name."

"It's your second name," he said gently. "Or so you told them. It was understood that you didn't want publicity. The newspapers would have had fun with all our haste."

She thought, *But why White Plains? Why not New York City*? She would have asked, but he was talking.

"Even now, it's been kept quiet, Tyl. Grandy and I agreed to that. Nobody knows except a very few. Oliver knows, of course, and Althea."

"Oh?"

Mathilda felt hysterical. It was so funny. What he was saying. Oliver, all this time—Oliver had thought her married to somebody else. So had Althea. Romance, tragedy, love and death, and Mathilda in the middle. All the while she'd been playing dull bridge with filthy cards, slapping at the flies, Althea had been believing this wild yarn. Mathilda put her thumb in, her mouth and bit it. It was too funny, too terribly funny.

"And as a matter of fact, that porter was bribed. He was bribed not to say anything about us. My dear, you bribed him yourself. That's what he thought you—"

Mathilda said, "Could I have a drink of water?"

He got her the drink quickly. He was watching her as if he cared how she felt.

She said, "But I got on board my ship at noon on Wednesday."

"You remember that?" he murmured.

"Perfectly," she snapped. She was annoyed at a little demon of glee that kept thinking of Althea, outdramatized. She put the glass down, feeling calmer. "I was quite alone," she said.

"When we got back here after the wedding," he said, "there was a message that I had to report immediately. We figured that it would be better for you to go on, that I would go see what the hell, do what I could. I was optimistic. I said I'd fly down after you. I even thought I might make it as soon as you did." He paused.

"I won't go into how I felt. I thought, after all, I had you legally, and for the rest I had, more or less, planned to wait—if you understand me." He sent her a queer, tortured glance. "But now it looks as if I haven't got you at all."

She took up the glass and tilted it. "Is there more?"

"Some," he said. "There was Grandy. You hadn't told him."

"Why not?"

"I think you rather liked the idea of a dramatic *fait accompli*, for Althea's sake."

Mathilda squirmed. He was making her out a blind little fool, a hurt, silly child. Her face burned because, although it wasn't true, it had a strange possibility to it, an accusing possibility.

"Well," he went along easily, "you didn't know what to do. Finally, you sat down and wrote him a letter—the last thing you did before I took you to the pier." He had a letter in his hand.

"A letter to Grandy?" She felt proud of being so rational. "How does it happen he hasn't kept it?"

"Because of what it says!" cried Francis impatiently. "My God, Tyl, you forget! We thought you were drowned. The letter was . . . all I had."

She thought, *I can't catch him. He always wiggles out with a sentimental answer*. She unfolded the letter.

The letter was not only in her handwriting; it was in her words. The turn of the phrases. There were even some that referred to family matters, such as saying "a Julius," when you meant a myth. An old story about a man named Julius who never came. Nobody could have known how to use that word! The letter was signed with her own cryptic formula. "Y.L.U.D. Your Loving Ugly Duckling."

"You took that to Grandy?" she asked, and her voice trembled. "He believed it?"

"Yes," said Francis gently. "Yes, of course. But I didn't take it to him until late in February. You see, the news about your disappearance came while I was still at camp. I got out of there so fast the red tape is still bleeding where I cut it." He grinned.

Her heart jumped. The grin was more terrifying than anything else he'd said or done, somehow. She realized that this was a man of great force, very much alive, a strong man, a consequential human factor. And here he was, claiming to have let his life and affairs revolve around her. Nor could she imagine any reason for it.

"I was frantic. I couldn't find you. Look, Tyl," he said boyishly, "what else could I do? I had to go where Grandy was, because if by any miracle you did turn up, you'd let him know. And listen, my darling—"

"I have been listening," said Mathilda. She raised her head. "Have I heard it all?" She stood up. "I don't know how you managed that letter," she said steadily, "but it's all lies, just the same." *Fight him*, her instinct said. "And I would like to see," she said boldly, "if you please, the man who married us."

He had been watching her intently. Now, when she lashed out, he didn't flinch. Instead, his face softened. "Good," he said. "I'll have the bags sent over to the station. We may just have time."

A maid in the corridor called her "Mrs. Howard." Mathilda stammered something. The clerk downstairs leaned across to say in a warm undertone, "Welcome back, Mrs. Howard."

Francis led her across the lobby. He was looking down, smiling a little, a smile not exactly triumphant, but rather as if he hoped she wouldn't be angry that he was right.

"You're very thorough," she said stiffly. But she was scared.

"The headwaiter?" he asked. "Shall we find him? Or shall we go into the bar?"

"No," she said. "No more, not these. . . . It was a minister?"

"It was a minister."

"I want to see him."

"I'd better phone," he said, and left her. The lobby floor was billowing a little under her feet. She thought, *He couldn't bribe a minister or make him lie.*

7

When Grandy opened the door of his study to go forth, Jane could see from her desk down the long room to where Althea was languidly dusting the floor. Althea wore a blue denim coverall and her silver-blond hair was tied up in a blue scarf. She wore gloves—dainty ones, too—and now Jane saw her fold her hands around the handle of the dust mop and lean picturesquely on it. Althea dusting the living-room floor was something to watch, a picture. Althea made the most of her opportunities in Grandy's servantless house. She never missed an opportunity to be a picture.

And Grandy, thought Jane, with his dramatic sense. It was like living in the middle of a movie all the time, to be in this house with the pair of them. The way he opened the door of the study. Not merely so that he could go through it into the next room. No, there had to be a flourish, a significant sweep. He opened the door as if he were blowing a fanfare for himself.

"Mathilda is in New York," he chanted, "even now." He seemed to be tasting each word. "I spoke to her on the telephone." The way he said it, the warmth and wonder he could pour out with that voice of his, made you reflect what a miracle the telephone was, pay mental tribute to Alexander Graham Bell, realize the strides of modern civilization, all in a flash, and then go on to consider the infinite pathos of human affection, and, somehow or other, also the gallantry of the human spirit in the face of the infinite.

Althea said, "Was Francis with her?" She had a clear, high voice. She articulated well through her pretty, small mouth, with a precise, rather strong-minded effect.

Grandy put his ten fingertips together in pairs, tapped his mouth with the long triangle of his forefingers. "Oh, yes," he said, "and I think . . . spaghetti!" The lines around his eyes crinkled up shrewdly. "I shall begin my sauce. Yes, spaghetti will be exactly right. Both friendly and delicious, but not distracting."

Althea made a slow, wide circle with the mop. "They'll be here for dinner," she remarked. It wasn't a question. It wasn't a comment. It was as if the thought in her mind had got expressed accidentally.

"Flowers!" cried Grandy.

"Let Jane do the flowers," Althea said. I'm just out of a sickbed. I decline to get my feet wet."

"The rain is only in your sulky little heart," said Grandy lightly.

Oliver, standing in the arch, asked suspiciously, "What rain? Whose heart?"

The minister's house was one of those city brownstones with a high stoop and a double-doored entry. The white lace curtains were spotless and crisp. The paint around the window frames was neat and newly done.

A servant opened the door. Her face broke into welcome. "Mr. Howard and your bride!" she said. "Oh, the doctor will be glad. I'll tell him."

She went briskly down the hall to tap on a door toward the back of the house. Francis was whispering in Mathilda's ear, saying that the servant had been a witness. To their wedding, he meant. Mathilda couldn't speak.

She felt the quiet of the house oppressing her. The very cleanliness, the spotless carpet, the shining wood of the stair banister, the faint smell of polish and soap, seemed inhuman and frightening. Somebody spoke from above.

A tiny elderly woman with soft, faded skin and faded blue eyes was standing on the stairs. "My dear," she said in a lady's voice, "we read in the papers that you were safe. How very kind and thoughtful of you to come."

The strange woman came all the way down into the hall and her hands touched Mathilda's. Her tiny hands were ice cold.

Francis said, apologetically, "She's been through a good deal, Mrs. White."

The woman's eyes narrowed. They looked at Francis very intently, very searchingly. They seemed to cling to his face, to pull away reluctantly at last. She whispered, "Poor child."

"She would like to see Doctor White," said Francis, and Mathilda had a strong sense that he was suffering.

"Of course," the woman murmured. They followed her in the track of the servant, who had vanished. This woman tapped, too, on the same door, and then she opened it. For a moment Mathilda could see only the outline of a man sitting behind a desk. He rose.

He said in a soft, powerful voice, "My dear Mrs. Howard—" He, too, came and touched both her hands.

Mathilda clutched. She was frightened. She found her fingers twined around his big hands as if she had been a child. She said, "I would like to talk to you by myself, please."

"Why, of course," he said with a certain tenderness. "Please, Hilda."

When they were alone, Mathilda said, "Doctor White, you aren't going to tell me that you performed any marriage . . . that I am the girl you married to—to Mr. Howard? Are you?"

His heavy brows lifted. "I am not likely to forget your face," he said. His eyes did not falter or change his odd look of sorrow. "You have a very beautiful face, my dear."

Mathilda was unbalanced a moment by such a strange and unexpected compliment to her appearance. Then she cried, "But I'm not the girl! If there was a girl! He's been trying to convince me, but I've never seen him before! I've never seen you! It isn't true! Please!"

He drew a book toward him and showed her the page. She saw the names again: John Francis Howard. Mary Frazier, written in her own hand. "No," she cried. She sank back in the chair and put her hands to her eyes.

"You are confused," said the minister in his soft, mellow voice. "That is a terrible feeling. I know. Won't you have faith that all will come clear to you in a while?"

She looked at him, startled. What was he trying to tell her? That she was mad?

"Try not to—dwell on it," he went on, with difficulty. "I don't think you can doubt your own senses."

"No," she said, stiffening. "I don't doubt them. And he can't make me. Nor can you."

"That's right," he said calmly. "Rest on what you remember, on your own best belief. My dear, if you are right and we are all . . . mistaken, for some terrible reason, then it must become clear sooner or later."

"But why?" she cried. "Why isn't it clear now? I'm not mistaken. I'm not sick. Why"—her voice rose hysterically—"why does everybody tell me this lie?"

He came around the desk and put his big hands on her shaking shoulders. "Remember this," he said at last: "I have known Francis before. I know that he has no wish to harm you, Mathilda. And you are not sick. Don't believe that for one second. Don't consider it." He walked away from her.

And the blood drained away from her heart in sudden panic because something about this man was familiar to her. He was a stranger, but some things about him she seemed to know.

"Come to see me again." He seemed distressed. He opened the door to the hall. The woman came and Mathilda felt herself being led away. The woman was talking softly about tea.

Mathilda was puzzled and angry and frightened, and comforted. She felt somewhere in this quiet house a secret, a secret to do with herself. She was comforted by a queer sense that if she knew she would understand. At the same time, she resented that there should be any secret.

"I won't drink tea here!" She flung it in the woman's face.

"Poor child," murmured Mrs. White.

When Francis and the doctor came belatedly through the door, she searched the minister's face for that sympathy. But his face had turned to stone. Even his eyes had changed. They no longer seemed to be seeing her. The sympathy and the mystery both were gone. He said, "I'm very sorry." But he was not. Not any more.

Mathilda thought to herself, *Don't make a scene. Don't cry. Get to Grandy. Grandy will know what to do.*

8

"Did you know Rosaleen Wright?"

She was startled. They had been sitting side by side on the train, like strangers. She said, "Of course."

"Did you like her?"

"Of course," she said again. "We are good friends."

"Were," said Francis.

"What?"

"She's dead, you know."

"I . . . didn't know," said Mathilda finally. She was shocked clear out of her own circle of thoughts. "What happened to her?" she asked quietly, in a minute. "Was she ill?"

"She hanged herself," he said.

Mathilda wanted to scream. "Is this another of your lies?" she managed at last. She thought she had never been so buffeted and shaken up and confused and shocked by anyone in her life. This man seemed dedicated to the business of upsetting her.

"Why should I lie about that?" he snapped back angrily.

She shook her head. She held up her hand as if to beg for an interval between the shocks he kept dealing. Rosaleen, who was such a dear, such a comfort, so much her friend, the only one Althea had never bothered to take away. Rosaleen, whose steady friendship she'd known and kept and never flaunted, lest Althea stir herself to spoil it. Rosaleen, who was so steady and so strong, couldn't be gone, couldn't have been driven desperate, couldn't have been so shaken—

"I don't believe it!" she gasped.

"Don't believe what?" He was eager.

"That she'd do that."

"Now, don't you?" he said oddly.

"No."

"That's the story," he shrugged. "She hanged herself five days after you were reported lost. In Grandy's study. She stood on his desk and—"

"Oh, no!" she cried. "Never!"

"You knew her well?" His voice was warm. He must have leaned closer.

"But tell me," she gasped, "why did she? Why?"

"No reason."

"What do you mean?"

"I mean there wasn't any reason."

"But there must have been! I don't understand! What a dreadful thing!" Mathilda wrung her hands. "Oh, poor Grandy!"

"Poor Grandy indeed," he muttered.

Something in his voice touched off her anger again. She leaned forward and twisted to confront him. "There you go again. Now, why do you say that?"

He looked up innocently.

"You don't like Grandy. What is it? What are you trying to do? There's no use denying. I can tell."

"Just a minute," he said, "before you go all intuitional on me. Why do I say 'Poor Grandy, indeed'? Because it strikes me you feel sorry for the wrong person. Poor Rosaleen! Don't you think?" He closed his eyes. "You don't even try to imagine what I might be feeling. Can't you tell? You fly off the handle about Grandy. He's the one." He opened his eyes and met hers boldly, almost impudently. "Can't you see I'm jealous of that old man?"

Mathilda bit her lip. "Maybe," she said in a queer, high little voice, "you and I are just two other people."

He didn't smile. He reached into his pocket as if he'd thought of something. Mathilda brought her eyes to focus on what he held. She saw her own face, laughing.

Francis was murmuring, "Not that it caught you. Two dimensions wouldn't be enough. The beauty you've got is pretty near fourth dimension. It's motion. It's time. It's what I said, like flying."

Her throat felt dry again. What he said was babble. But this was a picture of herself that she had never seen. She thought, *The camera doesn't lie*. Then she thought, *It's a trick*.

But for the first time her imagination did encompass the impossible, and she thought, just fleetingly, *What if all that he says is true? Nonsense. You might forget, but you don't invent another way of passing the same time and paste it over the gap in your memory.* She must get to Grandy. She must not look at anything any more.

When the train got in, he took her quickly to a cab. Mathilda felt a little sick and dizzy. She'd had no time to be prepared. How could she face Oliver? How could she find a way to think of him, a way to live her life in his physical presence?

Oliver had always been around. Such a nice guy, such fun, always around, always willing to go swimming, to play a little tennis. Always ready to gossip or just chat. Oliver had no driving energy toward a purpose of his own. Nothing ever interfered with his availability. What he did for himself, work, if any, was always done unobtrusively, of second importance in his scheme of things. He was always around. One grew to depend on it.

Oh, she thought, he would be there now. Married to Althea. How to face Althea? How to hide this as she had always hidden

Althea's power to hurt her? Ever since they were little girls, and Tyl's feet and eyes were too big for the rest of her, and she was unsure and shy, Althea, full of grace and pretty poise, had always been watching with her shining eyes. If Tyl had a friend or began an awkward progress toward something less lonely, Althea would manage to slip between and dazzle the friend away. Perhaps she never meant to do it. Perhaps she couldn't help it. No good. Tyl's heart wasn't ready for charity yet. How could she face them?

She was astonished to hear Francis say, "Take it easy, Tyl. He'll be feeling brotherly and a bit miffed. He thinks you're mine."

"Is Althea there?" she asked painfully.

He hesitated. Then he said, almost pityingly, "Why do you let Althea throw you? Don't you know she's envious of you? Always has been?" and while Mathilda gasped, he added savagely, "Althea's been tight in bed with la grippe, but she's up now."

Mathilda didn't understand that savage tone, she didn't understand him, but she felt softened toward him.

Grandy's portico. The big white front door.

Oliver said, "Well, Tyl!" He took her hand. He kissed her cheek. She felt nothing. The moment was blurred. There was Althea, standing back in the hall. She wore yellow. She was exquisite. Her oddly shining gray eyes weren't looking at Tyl at all.

A blond girl in a black wool frock who had the face of a baby doll smiled at her and went running down the long living room, calling, "Mr. Grandison!"

Tyl waited where she was for Grandy. She saw him coming—the arrogantly held gray head, the beak of a nose, the lively eyes behind the pince-nez, the unimpressive body with the fat little bulge of a tummy, the thin legs, the biggish, awkward feet.

She began to laugh and cry. He was purring. His beautiful voice that seemed not to need any breath came pouring out in endearments. Through her own tears, she could see in his black eyes the eternal spectator, who viewed with such lively interest and delight this dramatic and emotional moment in which he took part. He was just the same. She threw herself into his arms. She felt so safe. It was wonderful to feel so safe.

9

Never afterward was Mathilda able to put the finger of her memory on the moment that changed everything. It was like the tides on the beach. The sea would be coming up on the sand. Later, one was aware that it had begun to go down instead. But the moment of change escaped, couldn't be remembered, was not noticed at the time. So it was about Oliver.

There was a familiar hubbub. Grandy thought she was too thin. "My poor baby, your eyes are bigger than your face!"

Althea said, "That suit, Tyl!" with shocked disgust.

They introduced her to Jane Moynihan. Grandy had a visitor in his study who must be dismissed. He trotted off down the long room again. She saw Francis follow, saw him stop, halfway down, to speak to that pretty little girl named Jane. She saw Althea, watching.

Mathilda remembered later that she was able to turn easily and look Oliver square in the face, finding it the same friendly face, the same sandy eyebrows. Suddenly she could see the white walls of the African town in the sun. The waters of the oceans of the world were crisscrossed with the vanished tracks of the ships of men. She thought, *I've been away.*

He said, "Gosh, Tyl, you'll never know how I felt!"

She thought, *I'll never care.*

The tide had turned. It was going out. The strange thing was that it must have turned before this, and she hadn't known. But it was true; she didn't care any more how he felt, how he had felt or how he would feel tomorrow. The agony of caring was gone. Maybe she'd beaten it out of herself by caring so much and so hard. She felt very tired, as if all the sleep she'd lost over her emotions about him had accumulated in a reproachful cloud. It hadn't really been necessary.

Something must have gone out of her face, because Oliver could tell. She could see him persuading himself that he was, on the whole, relieved and glad. She saw right through. It was like watching the wheels go around in an insignificant toy. It was fascinating, but not important. Then the weariness lifted and Tyl felt free and lively. Her body felt light.

She said gaily, "Where are my things? Where do I go?"

"You're in the gray room." Althea was approaching with her mannequin's walk. "I'm afraid we took your old room, darling. Naturally, since it was always the nicest."

"Yes, I know," Tyl murmured. She was amused. It seemed to her that Althea was suddenly transparent too. Oliver picked up her suitcase. There was a little silence among the three of them, because Francis' two bags with his initials on them were there on the floor.

It came into Mathilda's head to tell them, then and there, and yet she didn't. She ought to have said, "I'm not married to Francis." But something was wrong with her mood. She couldn't have said it without giggling.

"Fran's been down in the guest house," Althea was saying.

"Oh, leave them," said Tyl carelessly. She was too much amused, too tickled, too giddy with inner mirth to tell them now. She ran upstairs. Her feet felt like flying. Althea came pelting after.

"Lord, Tyl, you are a skinny little rat."

Mathilda was burrowing into the gray room's clothes closet. She found a green wool dress. *In the eye of the beholder*, she thought. *In a pig's eye.*

"I've got good ankles," she said, muffled among the clothes. The knowledge that Althea couldn't hurt her made her dizzy.

Althea had sat down on the foot of the bed and her shining eyes that caught and reflected the light as if they had been metal, like silver buttons with black centers, were fixed on Tyl as if to read her very soul.

"What on earth happened to your hair?" she cried.

Althea's own hair was a soft silvery cloud of curls, cut short, swept up, every tendril blending charmingly with the whole effect. Mathilda shook her brown mane, which hung free to her shoulders. "I washed it myself," she said defiantly.

Althea's delicate eyebrows trembled with pitying comment. She touched the nape of her own neck with a polished finger tip. "I've been down with the grippe," she said, and sighed. "I've been miserable."

"Too bad." Tyl bit her lip. Laughter bubbled inside. She could hardly keep it under. *And I've been shipwrecked and rescued and half around the world, she thought, and it's eating you. Oh, it's eating you.*

Althea said, with grudging admiration, "You're a sly one." She sloped gracefully back on one elbow. "Where did you find this Francis of yours?"

Mathilda, in her slip, let her bare shoulders fall a little.

"A millionaire," complained Althea. Her voice verged on a whine. "Really, Tyl, you scarcely needed a millionaire. It doesn't seem just and fair. Look at Oliver and me, poor as church mice, both of us."

And it's eating you, thought Tyl. "I know what you mean," she said aloud, flippantly. "Maybe we ought to shuffle and deal again."

She saw, in the mirror, Althea's dainty body stiffen, saw the painted lashes draw down to narrow those gleaming eyes. *What ails me*? she wondered. She was treating Althea to a taste of sauce, as she had never dared before. She thought, *It's true. She is envious. She always has been.* She thought, *But I ought not to let her go on thinking I'm married. I mustn't be childish.*

She said aloud, "There's something you don't know about—"

"Is there, indeed?" said Althea acidly. "About true love, I suppose?"

Tyl picked up her own turquoise-handled hairbrush and made her mane fly. She thought, *Just for that, you can wait.* And again, suddenly, she wanted to laugh. Her mouth began to curve. She had to control it. The whole situation was so totally turned about. So ridiculously altered from what she had feared. For it wasn't Althea who had the husband Tyl had wanted. No. It was Althea who wanted the husband she thought Tyl had. Althea had her silver eyes on Francis.

10

INSIDE THE study, the man named Press waited. He stood looking down at the floor.

"Now, as I said," purred Grandy, "I don't intend to repeat such a broadcast. They came around, you know, and I had to claim a good deal of poetic license. But you needn't worry. You are still unsuspected. As I said. And don't come here. I'll be in touch with you from time to time."

The man had a very round head and wide-spaced dark eyes. He looked up. The eyes had no hope in them.

"Don't you know," said Grandy ever so softly, "I rather enjoy playing God?"

The man named Press barely nodded. His eyes were still hopeless.

Outside, in the living room, Francis smiled politely at the blond secretary. "Had to tell her the yarn," he said, as if he were saying, "Hello, how are you?"

Jane's pretty baby face was a perfect mask. "Oh, no," she moaned.

"Something's going to bust any minute. Pray I get hold of Althea before it does. Who's in there?"

"That man Press. The same one."

"I'm going to tell Grandy the duckling's lost her memory."

"Why?" Her pleasant smile might have been sculped on.

"For time," he said "To tempt him. Be ready to get out of here," he murmured, brushing by.

"Oh, Fran," moaned Jane.

Grandy's study door had a little whimsical knocker on the living-room side. It knocked back at you if the word was to come in. This was because the study had been completely soundproofed, so that Grandy's genius could work in quiet. Francis opened the door when the signal came.

"I thought you had company, sir," he said.

The visitor must have left by way of the kitchen. Grandy was sitting at his big light wood desk. He touched his pince-nez with his long-fingered, knot-knuckled hand. "No, no. Come in."

Francis walked across and sat down in the visitor's chair. He followed the precepts of good acting. He tried to think only of and within the frame of mind he was to seem to be in. He was a hurt, bewildered, rebuffed, humiliated and worried lover. At the same time, he mustn't miss anything he could glean from that face, that somewhat birdlike countenance, with its beak, its thin mouth, its black, brisk, bright and clever eyes.

"What is the matter?" asked Grandy, reacting promptly.

Francis looked up, surprised, looked down. "I don't know how to tell you," he mumbled. "I'm afraid I'm—" He rubbed his hand over his face, hoping it wasn't too theatrical a gesture.

Grandy stirred. He fitted a cigarette into his longish holder and slipped the holder into the side of his thin mouth. "Don't be tantalizing," he said. "What happened?"

Francis looked at him stupidly for a moment "I don't know," he said at last, roughly. "Mathilda doesn't—She says—"

"D'ya mean she's . . . out of love?" Grandy inquired.

"She was never in!" he flung back. "No. Worse. She doesn't know me."

"What do you mean?" Grandy didn't show any shock, except that the gray hairs on his head seemed to rise quietly, and stand straighter, at attention.

"I don't know," insisted Francis, "I suppose it's—I don't know what it is. She just plain doesn't, or can't, or won't remember me."

"How very extraordinary," said Grandy in a moment.

Francis was able to watch, somehow, without looking at him directly. He kept his own eyes down, and yet he knew that the expression on that face was alert and tentative. It was more plain curiosity and excitement than anything else yet.

Francis said, "I'm sorry. It just hits me, now. What am I going to do? I don't understand things like that."

"Do you mean you believe she is the victim of amnesia?" purred Grandy.

"Must be," said Francis. "Or whatever you call it. I don't know, sir. I don't know anything about anything. All I know is, I went to find her, and there she was and she didn't know me. She says she hasn't been hurt, or sick, or anything like that. I don't know what to think. I'm not thinking."

The hell I'm not, thought Francis. He got up and walked over to stare out of the window. It was a good thing to do, he'd found, when you were trying to think while being watched.

What did it matter any more how desperate this throw was? He was close. He knew nearly enough. There was such a little way to go. And if Althea hadn't taken to her bed with the grippe and if Oliver, with his ridiculous fuss, hadn't made it so plain that Francis was not admissible to the sickroom; if he hadn't been thwarted, delayed—why, he might have been finished by now, and able to come out into the open and let things burst. And if that little mutton-headed heiress hadn't jumped down his throat at the first word about her precious guardian, if he'd had the least hope that she wouldn't go blabbing immediately, if he'd been able to talk to her, tell her what he was doing, how much he knew, explain, ask her to help—

He saw now how foolish he'd been to think he could explain to her. To think that any perfect stranger could shake her deep-rooted faith in a man she obviously loved and adored. He might have known. Althea was the same. Bright-eyed Althea was blinded by Grandy. He knew better than to try to approach her with such frank and open tactics.

He wondered why he'd been led to think that Mathilda might be more approachable. Just hope. Just wishful thinking. Well, he'd seen quickly enough that it wouldn't work. And he hadn't wanted things to burst.

There was Jane for one thing. He'd made a mistake to mention her name. He hoped Mathilda wouldn't begin to wonder about that. No, he couldn't have confessed the whole crazy device then and there, and risked Mathilda rushing to a phone and risked Grandy finding out that Jane was . . . Jane. Not when Jane was here alone. Not when he had been too far away to stand between. Grandy was too smart. He could put two and two together too fast.

Well, it would burst now. Any minute. Unless, by this stubborn acting, he could muddle them enough. It was a nasty trick, a mean, cruel trick on the poor kid. Geoffrey had said so. Geoffrey hadn't wanted to go on with it. He'd been ready to balk. But when he saw how close it was, how sure Francis was now, and when he was reminded of Rosaleen—

Besides, sooner or later, the silly kid was going to be in danger herself. Blindly devoted to this evil old creature, she would never see what he was up to until too late. Wasn't it up to Francis, then, who knew all about it, to guard her, even from herself? Fancy thinking, maybe. A fine, high-minded excuse. There was some truth in it, although he didn't like it, didn't like any part of it.

But he had to make this desperate try. And at the back of his mind was the thought of the trap it set, the temptation. Grandy just might—just might pretend to be taken in long enough— After all, it would be very convenient for Grandy, in many ways, if there turned out to be something a little wrong with Mathilda's mind.

Grandy was being rather unnaturally silent. Francis turned around. He said, "What do you think? Ought I to fade out of the picture? Just to go away somewhere?"

Grandy was gnawing thoughtfully on his holder. His eyes were veiled. Francis thought, *He must be pretty sure I'm a fraud.*

Grandy said gently. "We certainly must do nothing at all in a hurry."

Francis fell a faint ripple of relief.

"She doesn't remember? She really doesn't remember?" Grandy crooned in his wondering way. "It's all gone out of her mind, you say? She feels she never saw you?"

Francis shook his head. He hoped he looked miserable.

"How very extraordinary," said Grandy again. "Poor duckling. Poor Tyl. You must have frightened her this morning. She's timid, you know, and shy, the little thing."

Francis thought, *Nonsense.* He'd fallen into the habit of checking this man's statements against his own evidence. It was very easy to let yourself go along with Grandy. You had to resist him. He thought, *I saw her spit fire. She's got plenty of guts. That yarn I told was well told. She might have gone to pieces. She isn't even little. She's a good-sized young woman.* Even so, the picture of Tyl, little, forlorn, pitiable, lingered in his mind.

He said aloud, "I tried not to frighten her. I will do exactly what you say, sir. Believe me, whatever you want me to do for Tyl's sake will be done, sir. Anything. Divorce?"

Grandy flicked him with a glance. Then he began to speak in his mellow, rich, butter-smooth voice: "How curiously we are made. Is it possible? The needle writes in the wax. The needle of life writes in the wax of the brain, and the record is our memories. Does the needle lift from the wax and leave no record? Or does a fog come down? What can we say? Do you know, I think the miracle is not that we sometimes can forget, but that we remember so much, so well."

Francis thought, *And I've got to get the record out of Althea's brain and play it back. He shook himself away from the hypnosis of Grandy's image. What is this? Is the old bird nibbling*?

"I do think," murmured Grandy, and Francis braced himself for the verdict—"I do think, dear boy, the wisest thing—" The soundproof room had a dead atmosphere. Sound behaved queerly. Silence closed in fast here. Grandy let a little hunk of silence fall. "—wisest thing to do is wait," he said.

Francis sighed. He couldn't help it. He hoped it would pass in character.

"Yes," said Grandy. "Let time pass. Let us wait and see. We will not inundate her with proofs or with evidence."

O.K. We won't, thought Francis. *But will you be checking on me some more*? He knew there had been some checking. Jane had been sent; Oliver had gone. Maybe others. Would Grandy check the story further or was he already sure that the whole fantastic untruth that Francis was telling was untrue? Francis thought, *I'm not fooling him. Can't be. Why does he bide his time, then? Because he doesn't know my motive? He wants to find out? The one thing he can't know is that I care about Rosaleen*. He thought, *Never mind why. Time is what I want*. He hardened his heart. Mathilda would have to suffer.

"Yes, let her rest," said Grandy. "Let her realize that she is safe at home."

Francis stood up. Safety wasn't a thing for him to think about. "Right," he said.

Grandy called him back with a motion of the cigarette holder. "Your marriage, as I understand it, was merely . . . legal?"

Francis said, "That's quite true, sir."

"You will stay on . . . in the guest house?"

"Naturally," said Francis.

11

GRANDY'S HOUSE stood on its own acre. It faced the westernmost street of the small city, a street that was almost like a country road, and its gardens spilled down a slope back of the house. Grandy said he had managed to have all the advantages of open country and yet escaped the need to do without city services. He claimed that his house was poised on the exact hairline of geographical wisdom. Grandy was full of theories about everything.

The house was not large. It was adapted to him. To the left of the hall ran his long living room, where he held court. On the south wall, a blister of glass was used for plants and porch furniture, and continued to the second story, where it became Grandy's exquisite and rather famous bathroom. His kitchen—another famous room—was directly at the back of the house. His study was not large—a one-story piece of the house tucked in between the kitchen and the living room. The dining room lay north.

He ran the entire establishment without servants. In the kitchen, he would preside over a collection of quaint copper pots, garlands of gourds, strings of onions, mixed in among all the latest gadgets in chromium and glass. He kept there a chef's hat which he wore seriously. Meals in his house were rituals in which the preparation of the food was just as important as the eating of it. He would bustle about and illuminate the proceedings with lectures in his fascinating voice. His lore, his stock of old wives' tales, was inexhaustible.

Mathilda came down in the green dress, and there he was in his cap, doing delicate last-minute things to the sauce. Oliver lounged against the wall. Francis was dusting glasses with a towel. Jane was setting the table.

Althea, on a high stool, was timing the spaghetti with Grandy's big round silver kitchen watch. She was still in her yellow gown—some soft silk with a wide skirt. She wore a lot of yellow. It was odd and striking on her. It gave a gold-and-silver effect and was arresting when black velvet would have been obvious.

Grandy came to embrace Mathilda. The big spoon waved back of her shoulder. He smelled of talcum and a little garlic. He beamed tenderly.

"Grandy," she murmured, close to his ear, "I need to talk to you. I have things to tell you." She knew it wasn't a good time, not with the sauce at the stage it was.

"I know," he crooned in her ear, "I know, dear, I know." Mathilda felt sure then that he did know. It didn't occur to her that he had been told, but just that he knew somehow. "After dinner," he murmured. "Let us be alone, eh?"

She was convinced that they must be alone while she told him. "Yes," she said eagerly, "alone."

He looked into her eyes. How anxious he was, how tender, how wise! Yes, he would know, of course. He sensed it already. She was quite safe. There was no hurry.

They trooped after Grandy, who carried the deep wooden bowl of spaghetti as if he held it on a cushion to show the king. But Grandy was the king too. There was candlelight Mathilda at his left, then Oliver. Althea at the foot. Then Francis. Then Jane. Happy family. Mathilda felt gay. No hurry; and, meanwhile, it was all so terribly amusing.

There was Oliver, on her left. A mild man, married to dynamite, and he didn't know what to do, she could tell. He was a mild man, a little man, in spite of his size, a drifting kind of creature, willing to be available and kind. But he didn't know what to do about the flagrant behavior of his bride. He fluctuated between stern anger and the determination to put his foot down, and another mood, a conviction of weakness and the tired thought that it didn't really matter.

But Althea, in all her glamour, was down at the foot, being a young matron with such amusing reluctance. And Francis, beside her, was looking very gloomy, very much subdued. Mathilda was glad to see it. She felt it was only just that he should have to sit at the table with the ax hanging over his head.

At the same time, she felt a surge of violent curiosity about him. What was the man up to, this Francis Howard? What kind of man? Well-bred, you could tell at table. Really quite attractive, if you liked that dark type, that lean kind of face. "Fortune hunter." She remembered her formula. She looked at his clothes. They were in expensive good taste. But if money wasn't his motive, what could it be?

She thought, angrily, as she'd been taught to, *All that stuff about my beauty.* She thought, *If he thinks he isn't going to be caught out in his lies— If he thinks I won't find out what's at the bottom of them—* She caught a suffering look from his dark eyes, and she smiled a little cruelly.

Francis asked Jane for the bread. The little blond girl looked as if butter wouldn't melt in her mouth. Tyl's green eyes took stock of her.

Nobody had even mentioned Rosaleen. Rosaleen was gone, although she had sat on Grandy's right hand in her day.

But they began to ask Mathilda questions, and she left off her puzzling to tell the tidbits she'd saved for Grandy. About Mrs. Stevens' drinking spells. About Mr. Boyleston and his one eye at the bridge table. All at once it seemed funny and rather gay. Besides, it burned Althea up.

Down at his end, Grandy listened. And his black eyes were restless and shrewd. Once he said, "Poor Tyl," in the middle of the laughter and watched her face sadden obediently.

Francis saw it too. He thought, *Damn it, the kid looks intelligent. Can't she see what he does? He directs her. Plays on her feelings like an organ, the old vulture.* The beautiful bones of Mathilda's face haunted and reproached him. He was miserably tense and unhappy. He wished the dinner were over. He wished he didn't have to sit here, looking soulful, when what he would really like to do was to smash in that beaming hypocrite's beaming face and snatch Mathilda and shake some sense into her, and then take Jane and get out of here. Damn such a game!

Althea's little foot was in his way under the table. He brought his own foot to rest, touching hers, and let it stay. Damn such a game, but if you have to play it, play it!

When Mathilda had done, Grandy went to work and changed the mood. He brought sea mist into the room, gray, fast, lonely danger, salty death. He made them remember the coral bones of those lost at sea. He told one of his favorite ghost stories.

Tyl began to look less vivid. She sobered and shrank. The wild mood, the free feeling ebbed away. After all, she was only poor Tyl, plain little Tyl, with all that money, who could never trust anyone very much. She'd have made a lovely ghost, a sad little green-eyed ghost with a broken heart and seaweed in her lank brown hair. She might have come to haunt them. She shivered a little. She saw Francis looking at her with scorn.

Scorn! From that quarter! She straightened her back. She said adoringly, “Oh, Grandy, it’s so good to hear you talk!”

Francis trod on Althea’s toe. “In the guest house. After dinner. Will you?” Her silver eyes were both surprised and delighted.

12

"I THINK they just stepped out, Mr. Keane," said Jane. Jane was the shy little outsider all the while, the one who made the obvious remarks and did the right thing.

Grandy looked at Mathilda, took the dish towel out of her motionless hands.

"Fine thing," Oliver said. He was trying to look very black. He seized on the state of Althea's health. "She had that cold. She oughtn't to be out."

Grandy said, "Poor Francis," gently, watching Mathilda.

She was wildly puzzled. Why was Grandy watching her so? What did it mean if Francis and Althea went out to the garden? Why "poor Francis"? Why Althea, anyway? She had a nightmarish feeling that the others knew what she did not know. She rejected it fiercely. Not so. It was she who knew and they who had been deceived. And the quicker she made it plain the better.

Grandy said, "Shall we—"

She thought he meant that they would talk now. "Yes, now," she said. But the doorbell rang.

"There now, answer the doorbell, Oliver. Please, dear boy. Who can it be?"

They went into the long room. Grandy took his chair by the

fire. Tyl took her low chair at his feet. Jane, who had followed them, went a little aside, picked up a bit of knitting and put herself meekly into the corner of a sofa. It was just as if Grandy had composed the picture, directed the scene. Even the firelight flickered with just the proper effect. Luther Grandison at home. Curtain going up.

Oliver came in from the hall. "It's Tom Gahagen."

Gahagen was the chief of the detective bureau, a small, lean, nervous man with a tight dutiful mouth, but a friendly face. He listened with an air of waiting, while Grandy enlarged charmingly upon Mathilda's miraculous return from the sea. Then he said, clearing his throat naïvely, "As long as I'm here, Luther, there are a few questions. I thought it would be all right just to drop in and talk it over. Didn't want to make it formal, y'understand?"

Grandy nodded. "About poor Rosaleen?" Then he appeared struck to the heart by his own forgetfulness. He took Mathilda's hand. "My dear child, forgive me. You don't know—"

"Francis told me," Mathilda said.

"That's your husband?"

Mathilda's eyes widened. She heard Grandy say smoothly, "Yes, yes, her husband. . . . What did Francis tell you, duck?"

"Just that she—" Mathilda couldn't continue. She was shocked because Grandy had said Francis was her husband. She'd had it in her head all along that Grandy, somehow, knew better.

Gahagen said, "Very sad, the whole thing. Sorry to bring it back to mind, but there's a point we've just come across. Funny thing, too."

Jane's foot in the small black childish shoe rested on the floor, but only the heel touched and the ankle was tight. No one could see Jane's foot. Her face was calm and her eyes cast down, watching her work.

"You remember," Gahagen went on, turning to Grandy, "that

day, along about early afternoon, some of the newsmen got in here?"

"Yes, yes."

"Took your picture?"

"Did they not?" sighed Grandy. "Yes."

Gahagen's eyes went to the mantel above their heads. "One of those shots was right here in front of this fireplace. That clock's electric, ain't it?"

"Yes, of course." Grandy's voice was sirup sliding out of a pitcher.

Gahagen said, "I'd like to have a look at your fuse box, Luther. Want to see what arrangement you've got in this house."

"Why, Tom?"

The detective slipped away from Grandy's bright and friendly gaze. He chose to explain all this to Mathilda. "You see," he told her, and she couldn't wrench her eyes from his plain, kind face, "the girl got up on Mr. Grandison's desk in there. You know his ceiling hook—the one he had put in for hanging special lights? She—er—used that, y'see, and stepped off the desk, like." Tyl felt sick. "Well, it isn't pleasant to think about, but she couldn't help it—kicking, y'know. Her leg got tangled in the lamp on his desk, pulled it over, wires came out of the bulb socket."

"So they did," said Grandy. He sounded politely puzzled.

"What we figure now," the detective said, "is that she must've blown a fuse. Blown a fuse when she kicked the lamp, see?"

"Is that possible?"

"Certainly. It's possible all right. Couple of bare wires, they're going to short-circuit. I'll tell you why we wondered. That electric clock up there was showing behind your shoulder in this picture, and it was all cuckoo. Gave the time wrong. It says twenty minutes after ten. And the picture was taken after two o'clock in the afternoon. We know that."

"The clock was wrong?"

"Lemme look at it, d'you mind?" The detective got up to examine the black, square modern-looking clock. "Yeah, see? This one is the old kind. It don't start itself."

Mathilda was near enough to Grandy to feel him suppress an impulse to speak. Oliver spoke up impatiently. "No. of course it doesn't. You have to start it after the current's been off. The new ones start themselves."

"Anybody cut the current off that morning?" asked Gahagen. "Was the master switch thrown at all, d'you know?"

Oliver said "Not that I know of."

"Nor I," said Grandy. He edged forward in his chair. "I'm not sure that I follow you, Tom. What are you getting at?"

"Gives us the exact time," the detective said. "That is, if it does. Y'see, there was no power failure that day anywhere in town. We've already checked on that. So it must have been something right here in the house made the clock stop, see? Now I'd like to look at your circuits, eh? If this clock actually is hooked in on the same circuit as the study lamp, why—"

Again Grandy suppressed something. Tyl had a telepathic flash. Who'd told Gahagen about the clock and the circuits? The kind of clock it was, what circuit it was on? Because he wasn't wondering. He was checking.

"I don't understand," purred Grandy, "about the clock. But something's wrong with your thought, you see, Tom, because the lights worked."

"Yeah, we know." He nodded. "Lights were O.K. when we got here. So there's this question: Did anybody put in a new fuse?"

Oliver was looking blank.

"If so, who?" said Grandy softly. "Fuses don't replace themselves. I really—"

"They don't," said the detective. "If a fuse'd been blown, somebody knew it. Somebody replaced it. None of my men did." He waited, but no one spoke. "Well I don't suppose it's important. Still, I oughta—Where's your fuse box? Cellar?"

"Oliver, show him, do. . . . Jane, dear—"

Mathilda held on to Grandy's knee. The lights were going off and on all over the house. It was queer and frightening. Jane had gone to stand at the top of the cellar steps and call out which lights went off and when, while the two men below were playing with the fuses. Mathilda held on to Grandy's knee, which was steady. She had begun to cry a little.

Grandy was talking to her. He stroked her hair. ". . . nor will we ever know. Poor child. Poor, dark, tortured Rosaleen. She was so very tense. Tyl, you remember? Remember how her heels clicked, how quick and taut she was? Remember how she held her shoulders? Tight? Brittle, you see, Tyl. Strung too tight. Poor little one. No elasticity, no give, no play. And since she couldn't stretch or change, she broke."

"But why?" sobbed Tyl. "Oh, Grandy, what was wrong?"

"Not known," he said, like a bell tolling over Rosaleen's grave. "Not known. She didn't let us into her life, Tyl. You remember? She was with us and of us, but she was, herself, alone."

That's true, Tyl thought.

"I think it was in the air," he continued. "The house was waiting, days before. The storm in her was disturbing all of us, but we didn't know. Or we put it down to sorrow and suspense over you, my dear. But now I remember that morning. She was writing a letter for me, and the typewriter knew, Tyl. It was stumbling under her fingers, trying to tell me. I felt very restless. I didn't know why. Althea was fussing with a new kind of bread. She was in the kitchen, I remember. I felt the need of homeliness. I wanted to smell the good kitchen smells. Instinctively, I left her, Tyl." He paused.

"And of course, since it was rather a fascinating thing Althea was trying to do—cinnamon and sugar and apples in the dough—I became enchanted with the process. I'm afraid we forgot about Rosaleen behind the study door. Alone in there. Oliver was with us. The three of us were happy as children." His beautiful voice was full of regret and woe. "But there is a fancy bread of which we shall not eat, we three."

She sobbed. "When—how did you—who?"

"It was Oliver who—" he told her gently. "Noontime. He opened the door to call, and there was that little husk, the mortal wrappings—"

Mathilda whimpered. She heard the men coming back, Oliver and Gahagen. Jane too. She wished they wouldn't yet She wanted Grandy to say one thing more, something, anything to reconcile this tragedy, to heal it over, not to leave her heart aching.

"Well, it's on the study circuit, all right," said Gahagen mildly. He walked over and looked at the clock. "But you tell me nobody put any new fuse in?"

Grandy didn't repeat his denial. He sighed.

"Maybe somebody did and said nothing about it," suggested Gahagen.

"Possibly."

Oliver said, "But who? After all, we don't have servants, you know."

"Funny."

"Could the clock have been out of order?" offered Jane timidly. She was back in her corner. Her blue eyes were round and innocent, and wished to be helpful.

"It's running now," Gahagen said, frowning at it. "Who started it again after that morning?"

"By golly, I did!" cried Oliver.

"When?"

"Let me see. That night. I noticed it, set it and gave it a flip. Never crossed my mind till now."

"Don't sound like it was out of order. And it's on that circuit, all right. Kitchen, study, and this double plug, backed against the study wall. That's the fuse that went with the desk lamp when she kicked it over."

Grandy shook a puzzled head. He said wistfully, "I find mechanical contrivances very mysterious. Believe me, Tom, they are not always simply mechanical. They have their demons and their human failings. My car, for instance, has a great deal of fortitude, but a very bad temper. The oil burner is subject to moods, and the power lawn mower is absolutely willful."

Gahagen laughed. He said in a good-humored voice, "I don't want you to think we're snooping around after one of those unsuspected murders of yours, Luther."

"Oh, Lord," said Grandy humorously.

Jane turned her ankle over convulsively. Her heel clattered on the floor. She stopped knitting to look hard at the stitches.

"It's just that it was funny and we kinda wanted to check. Er—this Mr. Howard, he—er—wasn't here at that time, was he?"

"No" said Grandy. "No." His black eyes turned behind the glasses, slid sidewise in thought.

Gahagen frowned. "Have I got this straight, Luther? Now, when he came here, he was a stranger to you?"

"To me," said Grandy, "he was an utter stranger."

Oliver said, "Nobody knew him except Tyl." He said it with smiling implications.

Tyl opened her mouth to say, "But I didn't. I don't." She felt Grandy's hand on her shoulder. It said, *Be still.* She thought immediately, *No, no, of course, not now.* She leaned heavily against his knee.

"Where's Mrs. Keane?" asked Gahagen.

Grandy stepped smoothly in between Oliver and the answer. "She's gone out, I'm afraid. Unfortunately," he purred, "I scarcely know when to say she'll be in."

Oliver looked up, and then down. He pretended to be busy with a cigarette.

Grandy purred on, "But of course, in the morning—Suppose I ask her to drop in to see you at your office, Tom? Will that do?"

"Good idea," said Gahagen. "Yeah, do that. Couple of things I'd like to ask her. Maybe she changed the fuse."

"Oh, I doubt that," Oliver laughed.

"Well, if you'll ask her to stop by, that's fine. That'll—er—ahem." He cleared his throat.

It had all been between two clearings of his throat, like quotation marks.

When the detective had gone, Oliver said, "He was looking for fingerprints on that fuse. Now, why? What's the fuss about, do you know?"

"Dear me. Were there any fingerprints?" Grandy asked.

"No. Those milled edges won't take 'em. What is the meaning of all this?" Oliver looked alert. He wanted to hash it over. He liked to gossip.

Grandy looked up. "Eh? God bless us every one, I don't know, Ollie." Grandy sounded tired and sad. "Alas, I do not—I will never understand the ins and outs of electrical matters. I have not put my mind to them, don't you see?" There was something petulant in the statement, something childish, as if he were saying, "I could have if I'd wanted to. I did not choose to know."

"Althea couldn't change a fuse," said Oliver. Then his face rumpled up in the firelight. "Why didn't you call Althea, Grandy?" he asked uneasily.

Mathilda remembered with a start that Althea was only outside in the garden or in the guest house. Surely not far. She had no wrap. She had only slipped out for a moment. She couldn't have gone far. She looked at Grandy for his answer.

He said flatly, "It would have looked odd, I thought. I'm sorry, Oliver. After all, Althea out with Francis at this time—" He was looking at Tyl.

Yes, it was at least odd. Here sat Francis' bride, by his own reckoning, and only tonight was she returned from the sea. And where was Francis? Off somewhere with Oliver's bride. Or was Althea, as usual, after that which she had not? Or was Francis after Althea?

"You're damned right," growled Oliver, playing the he-man. His fingers did dramatic things with his cigarette. "It's plenty odd. Where the devil are they?"

Mathilda straightened her back. It was odd, but she ought not to feel annoyed just because she didn't understand. "Grandy," she begged, "can't we talk now? Alone, I mean. Please, darling, it's important."

13

Down in the guest house, Grandy's charming little cabin-style nook at the bottom of the garden, Althea was lying on the couch before the fire. Francis had put her there, put her feet up, touched a match to the kindling, set his stage. Now she was waiting. Her yellow skirt rippled off to the floor. The ruching at her neck made a deep square. She knew she was lovely. Her silver eyes still held the same expression of pleased and shrewd surprise. He knew he was nervous and too eager, and afraid to startle her with his need for haste.

"Althea." She moved her body in toward the back of the couch, folded in the cascade of her skirt with one quick gesture, making room for him to sit down. His face was above her. She let her lashes hide that pleased and wondering look. The ruching moved with her breathing. "Help me, will you?" Her darkened lashes lifted. "I've got a problem," he said. "Did you ever wonder," he went carefully, "why Rosaleen Wright did what she did?"

Althea looked disappointed. He groped for some way to interest her.

"I have an idea. I may have found out something—"

No flare. She was looking at him rather more coldly. To touch Althea, you touched what? Her vanity. Her jealousy.

"—about someone," he stumbled.

"Who?"

"Not Grandy," he lied quickly. He dared not make that mistake now. "Not Oliver," he added. He saw her mind scrambling behind the silver eyes. And in his need was able to follow it. She gave him the cue herself. "Someone else," he said lamely. There was only one person else, and her face was lighting up. "Help me," he begged. "I can't tell you more now. It would spoil what I want you to say."

"Me to say!"

"Listen." He took her hand. "Life is a needle. It writes on wax. Your memory's got a record. And I want to play it back. Will you try, Althea?"

"My memory?"

"Only you," murmured Francis. "And that's a bit ironical, isn't it?" He gave her his self-mocking look. "It means a good deal to me," he confessed. "Something I've got to know."

He thought, *I'll mystify her. I'll give her romance. I'll give her drama.*

Althea raised her shoulders from the pillow. "I thought there was something queer between you and Tyl. I thought she didn't seem—you didn't seem— What is it? What did you find out?"

Francis turned his face away to keep it an enigma in the face of this.

"Maybe she didn't go to Africa," whispered Althea. It was venomous. "I thought the whole thing sounded phony. The little fraud! People with one eye and all that junk!"

Francis wondered what to do now, with this thrust of her imagination in the wrong direction. Use it. Use it, if he could.

He said, "It's the morning Rosaleen died. I want you to go back and remember. Everything. Whether the phone rang. Did you hear a sound? Did anyone come to the house?" He threw ideas at her. Mix her up. Never mind what she thought. Make her talk. There wasn't much time. She had to talk tonight, in this hour.

Althea said, "But that hasn't anything to do with—"

"You mean, she was drowned by then?" said Francis bitterly.

Althea's brows drew together. He got up and poked the fire. Let the woman think any wild thing, only let her tell him.

She said very meekly, "I don't understand. What is it you want me to do?" She tilted her head back to lengthen her long white throat.

He told himself, *Go easy. Forget that any minute somebody from the house may come down to see where we are. Pretend there's time. Make the most of this chance.* She was willing, for this moment, and she was thrown off the real track by her jealous wish that Mathilda be somehow damaged. But she wouldn't go deep enough or carefully enough unless he held her to the detail he wanted.

"Do you remember getting up that day?"

"Yes."

"Breakfast?"

"Yes."

"With whom?"

"Grandy, Oliver, Rosaleen."

"What did you have to eat?"

"Good heavens, Francis—"

"You can remember, if you try. I want you to try. Because of something later."

"Because of what?"

"I can't tell you until afterward," he evaded.

"But there isn't anything," she said.

He leaned down, took both her hands. "Althea, please."

"All right. Coffee, toast, marmalade. That's what we had for breakfast."

"Go ahead. Play the record for me. Then what?"

Althea closed her eyes. Her fingers tightened on his. "Breakfast," she murmured. "Then it was Oliver's turn to do the dishes. I did the downstairs. Rosaleen made beds. Grandy ordered on the phone. Rosaleen came down and went into the study with him. Is this what you want?"

"Go on. Little things."

"Oliver went downtown. He kissed me and went out by the front door. He had galoshes on. One of them flopped." She was smiling, exaggerating the details. Good, let her. "Let me see. I vacuumed. I had the radio going."

"What program?"

"News," she said.

"What station?" Radio gives times. His pulse was faster.

"Heavens, I don't know. But then the Phantom Chef came on. He talked about bread. I wanted some. I went out to the kitchen and got out his book—"

"Got out his book," droned Francis.

"Had a pencil," she went on dreamily. "Checked the recipe. Got out a bowl, flour in the canister on the table. I was looking in the icebox for what it took."

"Did the light go out?" He held his breath.

"Go out? Light? Oh, the icebox light? Yes, it was out."

"You didn't see it go out?"

"No, but it was out. How did you know?"

"Go on."

He'd broken the spell. Maybe a mistake.

"Grandy came out of the study," she said slowly, still puzzling over that accurate guess. "He was talking over his shoulder to Rosaleen. He couldn't hear."

"Why couldn't he hear?"

"The radio," she said impatiently. "I had it up loud."

"Radio in the living room?"

"Yes, the kitchen end. I turned it down. He said what he had to say, and she answered."

"You heard her voice?"

"Yes." His heart sank. "No," said Althea. "Why?"

Was she defensive? Be careful.

"It was her voice, I mean."

"What?"

"No, no, I'm wrong. Not then." He struck his forehead. "Of course not, because Grandy was there. Wait now. Rosaleen answered or you thought she answered."

"I thought she answered," said Althea carefully, "and she did answer, because Grandy said to her, 'That's it, dear.'"

"Then?"

"I went back."

"You were still at the radio?"

"Yes. I turned it up again." Her thoughts seemed to stick at something. Francis dared not interrupt her now. A log fell in the fire. Flames murmured over it "Burn tenderly," said Althea.

"What—was that?"

"Burn tenderly." Althea smiled. "That's exactly what he said. It sounded so silly, blurted out loud without the context. He's pretty precious, anyhow. He can't do it the way Grandy can; although, of course, he tried to imitate."

"Who?"

"The man on the radio."

"Who said, 'Burn tenderly'?"

"The Phantom Chef. He did. That's the way he talks."

"He said 'Burn tenderly,'" said Francis gently. "Go on. Grandy had just, what?"

"Closed the study door." She shut her eyes again. "I said, 'I'm making bread.' I don't remember every word we said."

"Doesn't matter."

"I showed him the icebox light. He said it was the bulb. He'd fix it."

"Did he?"

"Fix it? Yes, I guess he did."

"Did he go down cellar?"

"To get the apples?"

"Yes."

"Yes, he got the apples. Oliver came home. We put the dough together."

Francis thought, *Don't let her see the trail. Don't let her see the point. Don't let her realize what she's told me.*

"Now!" he said breathlessly, and she tensed. "Did the phone ring?"

"No. No-o."

"Any bell?"

"No."

"Did you—was there a draft?"

"Draft?"

"Current of cold air."

"I don't think so."

"Someone came in the front door?"

"I don't know."

"Might have?"

"If it wasn't locked," she said.

No need to keep on with this any longer. He'd got what he wanted and covered it up enough.

"What is it?" she demanded. "What are you thinking?"

He shook his head. Althea said tartly, "And now you're going to be a little gentleman and tell no secrets."

Francis grinned at her. "That's right."

She settled back on the cushions. "Tell me something," she

asked lazily. "Are you as much in love with Tyl as you . . . made out?"

He let his eyes look startled, and make a tiny negative sign. He felt he owed her that. He turned to the fire. He was thinking he'd have to send Jane in to New York tomorrow. That meant one night more. He was thinking he'd better remember to be dejected, not let excitement show. For the old man was keen.

What Althea was thinking, he neither knew nor cared. Her hand was warm in his, and from time to time he pressed it. He was thinking of Mathilda. A little while and he could explain to her and beg her pardon. He could explain why he'd had to go into that song and dance about love. Because the story made no sense without it. He'd explain. Then he was thinking of Rosaleen, of her gallant little figure that seemed to diminish with the days, as if she were traveling away from him toward a horizon beyond which she would someday vanish entirely. He was thinking that sometimes she seemed to be looking back at him. But when it was done, when he had finished this task, then she would turn her face away forever.

14

"GRANDY, CAN'T we talk now? Alone, I mean. Please, darling. It's important." Mathilda hadn't seen them come in.

"What's important?" drawled Althea.

Oliver turned around to look at her, and his face flushed vividly with anger. Francis was a dark background, where the firelight and the lamplight barely touched him, as they stood there, just inside the room from the kitchen.

"Where have you been?" exploded Oliver. Her insolence set him off. The anger was genuine.

"Oh," said Althea, "talking."

"Talking about what?"

"Nothing worth repeating now," she said, and yawned daintily. "I do think I'll go up to bed," she said in the awkward silence. "After all, my first day out of it."

"Yes, do," said Grandy hastily. "Do, dear."

Jane got out of her chair. Mathilda thought she saw a glance pass between Jane and the white blur of Francis' face. "I think I'll say good night," said Jane primly. "Good night, Althea. Miss Frazier. Mr. Grandison, Mr. Keane." She murmured all their names politely.

All but one. She forgot to say good night to Francis. Mathilda thought it was odd. There was something in that forgetfulness that assumed he was different; either he didn't matter, or he would understand, or, thought Mathilda, he mattered most. Nobody else seemed to notice. Nobody else seemed to notice that she'd said "Miss Frazier."

"Good night," they said to Jane, raggedly.

Grandy said benignly, "Good night, child."

Jane showed them all her pretty smile and went away, withdrawing from the family, sweet, pretty and dutiful.

Althea stood where she was, looking strange, as if she'd been only half waked out of a hypnotic state or as if she were sleepwalking.

"Good night, Althea," said Francis. His voice had no caress or even much meaning.

"Good night," she murmured.

Oliver said, "Good night, all." He hadn't even a special word for Tyl, the returned one. He didn't even look at Francis. He was furious. His fury had a female quality. Oliver was in a tizzy.

"Now, Oliver," said Grandy with remarkable clumsiness.

Oliver bared his teeth as if to say "Keep out of this." He took his wife's arm to pull her along, but his hand slipped. The gesture was pitiful and ineffective.

"Oh, Oliver, don't grab at me," said Althea crossly.

"Very well," said Oliver. He was shrill. Tyl wanted to hide her eyes.

Althea swayed a little, standing there, looking down at Tyl. She wasn't very tall, but she looked tall at that moment, and slender, and mysteriously malicious. Tyl's heart contracted with a little fear.

Althea laughed softly. "Well, Tyl, you're back, aren't you? All the way back."

She bent her silver head and Grandy kissed her. She walked down the long room, vanishing into the dark at the far end. In a moment, Oliver snapped on the light in the hall and she was outlined in brilliance briefly. Then she was gone.

The three of them, by the fire, were silent until Francis threw his cigarette into the flames decisively.

"I'll go back to the guest house now," he said, with no emphasis at all. Tyl looked at him, but his face was turned away.

Grandy said softly, quickly, "Yes, yes, of course. For tonight."

Mathilda got up. She didn't know whether she wanted to run or fight it out now and smash that lie, this heroic suffering pose of his that lied so expertly. She looked at him with her anger and her suspicion and her resentment and her defiance in her eyes. But as he moved closer, she didn't shrink away. It came to her that she was not afraid of him. She would enjoy a good fight, a good, bold, hard-hitting clash.

"Don't run," he said surprisingly. But when he stood over her very close, although he didn't touch her, she could tell that he wanted to, and not so much with love as with pity. "Good night, dear," said Francis. He sounded sad. They were not fighting words. The words were lonely.

Mathilda still stood there when he had gone. She couldn't understand. Couldn't understand. The only thing that explained him was the lie he told. If he really were in love—But he was not! He was a stranger.

"Grandy."

Grandy was all huddled in his chair. He looked shrunken up, his hand shaded his eyes.

She knelt down swiftly. "Grandy, what is it?"

"This house," he said. "Tyl, is it talking? Do you feel . . . something wrong?"

Her throat tightened. She cast a quick look behind her.

"I don't like it." Grandy rocked his shoulders. "Oh, no, I don't like it."

Tyl said, "Grandy, there's nothing. But there's something I've got to tell you."

He pulled himself up and smiled then. His hand came to cover hers warmly. "Darling, I know. I must lock the doors. Run up, sweet. I'll come. I'll tuck you in, eh?"

She nodded. She went upstairs slowly, grasping the banister too tightly. She could hear Grandy below, moving briskly, locking the doors. Whatever the mood had been, he'd thrown it off. And this was her home. Surely it was safe here. There could be nothing here to fear.

She went into the gray room and found the switch, but she didn't press it. She crossed quickly to the window in the dark. Was that a sound?

Outside, the night was not too deep for her to see a figure in the garden. Was it only this morning, she wondered, that she had first seen that figure, that man's shape? Only today?

The sounds were faint. She knelt and hid her head behind the curtain. She could see another figure, climbing down the trellis from the roof of the kitchen porch. Only she could see it, only from this room. Climbing down! Out of Rosaleen's old room to the porch roof, of course. That Jane! Her blond head caught a little light from the sky. The two figures met and shimmered in the dark and seemed to dissolve into shadows.

Tyl sat back on her heels. "My noblehearted lover!" she said. "My suffering bridegroom! Oh, brave good lonely soul!"

15

"JANE." FRANCIS held her by the shoulders. He spoke in a low tone that wouldn't carry. His face was just a blur. "You've got to go to New York tomorrow." He shook her with his impatience. "Make it your day off. Disappear and leave a note. It doesn't matter if he doesn't like it. Get away early."

"What do you want me to do?"

"I've got it!" he croaked triumphantly. "I finally got Althea to talk about it. Listen, see if you don't get the point. We know the clock stopped at twenty after ten." He let go of her shoulders.

"Fran, I've got to tell you—"

"Not now. Wait. So the fuse blew at twenty after ten that morning. Now Althea says that Grandy came out of the study and was closing the door of it behind him at the very minute when the Phantom Chef fellow was on the air—the one who gives out recipes, you know, Jane. She remembers something he said. Jane, it gives us the time! Don't you see?"

"I see. I think I do."

"The fellow said 'Burn tenderly.' Remember that. Two words. Write them down. They take records of those programs. They must have taken a record of this one. Pray they have. You've got to go to the radio station and find out. Maybe they took a record there.

Or if they didn't, sometimes the client does. Find out who pays for that program. See if they took a recording. Try the advertising agency. Try everywhere. Find that record, Jane. And then make them let you listen. Make up a yarn, anything. Don't you see? If you can listen, and time the thing, and spot the very minute when he said, 'Burn tenderly'—"

"Uh-huh," said Jane. "Uh-huh."

"That'll be the proof we're looking for. Proof! If the time is different from what I expect, then we're all wrong, and we'll know it. Jane, we can't be wrong. And if those words were said on the air that morning any time—even seconds—after twenty after ten, then we've got him! Got enough to go to the police. Because that would mean she was dead—" He drew away in the dark. "Oh, God, Jane, she kicked that lamp over while she was dying, and he stood there watching her!"

Jane said, in a minute, grimly, "That'll do it."

"Yes," he repeated wearily, "that'll do it."

"I'll go into town. I'll find out." She might have been taking her oath.

"Yes, you go in." He wished the night were over. He wished it were morning.

Jane said, "Fran, Gahagen was here."

"What?"

"Yes, and I—"

"What did he want?"

"He was asking all about the clock. He looked at the fuses too."

Francis groaned. "Did he say how the police came to be wondering about that?"

"No, he didn't say. But I think he knew, all right."

Francis groaned again. "The old man is keen. Damn! Why did this have to happen tonight?"

"How do you suppose Gahagen knew that you were the man on the telephone?"

"They could have traced the call. I couldn't help it. I had to check; had to know whether the police had found a blown fuse or noticed—"

"They never would have noticed," said Jane loyally. "You found the newspaper picture with the wrong time on the clock."

"But I wish Gahagen hadn't shown up tonight."

"Fran, what's the difference? We've got it now. All we have to do is check."

"Yes," he said.

They were whispering in the lee of a great mock orange. The night was still around them. Chilly. Francis shivered. His scalp crawled. He wished it were morning and Jane on her way.

"Fran, tell me." She clutched at his arm. "What about Mathilda? What happened?"

"Mathilda doesn't matter," he said desperately.

"But what did you tell Grandy? What did he say?"

"I told him she was balmy. He—I don't know. I imagine he's wondering, right now, what I'm up to."

"You don't think he believed you?"

"No, I don't think he believed me," said Francis bitterly. "I'm good, but I'm not that good. I think he doesn't understand and he's lying low. I hope he doesn't get his mind clear until tomorrow."

"Poor Mathilda," breathed Jane.

"Tough on her," he admitted. He could tell Jane. "But, honey, what could I do? Go on trying to tell her that old precious is what he is? And have her run to him with all we've got, so far? So he could block any move we'd try to make? Don't think he couldn't. Or could I bow out and say, 'That's right, ma'am. I'm lying. Must have had a brain storm. So long.' And leave the job unfinished?

When we were so close? I couldn't do a thing, Jane, but what I did. I felt like a heel."

"She must have been staggered."

"She's got a lot of fight; she can take it. She's got to! A few confusing days. Jane, how the old man's got those girls under his spell! Svengali business. I don't like it. He's had Mathilda thinking she's a poor little unattractive dumb bunny for years and years."

"She's not," said Jane dryly.

"She's certainly one of the most beautiful creatures—" said Francis irritably. "But no, she'll take his word for it! I don't think she knows, herself, what she is, or ever will know until she gets away from him."

"So if we get him, she'll be free."

"Yes," he said. "That's the only way I can look at it."

There was a slam of sound. Somebody had slammed the back door. They froze in the shadows and turned their faces furtively. Someone with a flashlight went around to the garage. The overhead doors rolled up. In a moment or two, they heard a car start. It was Oliver's. It plunged down the drive and they heard the gears clash, as if the hand that shifted was in a mood for bangs and clashes.

"Oliver?"

"But what—where's he going?"

"Hell for leather. I don't know." Francis took a step as if he would follow and see.

"He was simply furious with Althea. They must have had a fight."

"Quite a fight," said Francis.

The car's noises died away, leaving the night to its old chilly quiet. Jane shivered this time. "Better get back." She turned to look at the quiet house that had just erupted and spit out an angry man, and now lay biding its time, to explode again with some evil or other.

"Yes, you'd better," said Francis with sudden urgency. "Look here, we forgot something. Grandy may not know about the radio voice, but he does know one thing. I should have seen that. He knows the icebox light went out when the fuse blew. He knows, because Althea told him. That's what tipped him off, in the middle of the morning, that a fuse had been blown. He trotted right down cellar and fixed it. Now, she didn't see the light go out—"

"If it was out," said Jane. "And if it was really Rosaleen's death that put it out, Fran, haven't we got proof already? Can't we use that? Use it now, tonight?"

"No, because it might have been the bulb burning out, after all," said Francis wearily. "He'd wiggle out that way. Jane, I—"

"What's the matter?"

"God knows what he'll do!"

She trembled. "What?"

"I hate to ask you to lose sleep when you have so much to do tomorrow. Jane, watch Althea's door."

"Watch?"

"Because Oliver's gone," said Francis. "Oliver isn't there. She's alone. And Gahagen's tipped off Grandy. Get into the house, Jane. It's not— I don't think it's safe."

"You don't think he'd— Not Althea!"

"No?" said Francis. "Rosaleen was young and pretty, wasn't she?"

Jane said, "Oh, Fran!"

"If you see anyone," he told her, "flash your lights. I'll be around."

As one, they turned and almost ran into the darkness to the kitchen porch. He boosted her up the trellis. Mathilda's window was dimly lit. The house stood whitely over Francis. The night, he thought, was getting colder.

16

"Now," said Grandy, "now we're cozy." He sat in the big yellow chair, and Tyl put herself on the yellow ottoman at his feet. They were together in a little pool of light from the tall lamp over them. The room was warm. It had an expensive smell. She'd had time to get out of the green dress and in to her own long warm robe of rose-colored wool. The soft fabric felt luxurious along her neck and arms.

"What's troubling you, duck? Now you shall tell me all about it."

"Just that Francis is a liar!" she burst out promptly. "A terrible liar, Grandy. I don't know the man! I never saw him before! The story about my having met him and got married to him—it's not true! Every bit of it is just made up. Because I remember exactly what I did in New York those three days. And he wasn't in it. So it's all a big elaborate lie!"

Grandy's black eyes narrowed.

Mathilda felt her temper rising. "Just about the biggest mess of lies I ever heard!" she cried. "Why, he had the bellhops and the hotel people all primed to say they knew about it. Even the minister, Grandy. And that letter to you! I never wrote any such letter. I couldn't have. Because it didn't happen. And that license business in the wrong name. It's just a fake! It must be!"

"Hush," he said.

"But you believe me? You do? Don't you?"

"Of course I believe you, Tyl," he said "Of course, darling. Hush."

She sagged forward, put her arms on his knees and her head down. "But did you ever hear of such a thing? Why it's—" She wanted to cry.

"Extraordinary," said Grandy. "It's perfectly wild, Tyl."

"I know!" she cried. "I couldn't make a fuss! I had to get home! Grandy, what in the world can we do about it?"

"To think he fooled me," Grandy said sadly. "To think he fooled us all."

"Oh, darling, I suppose you couldn't help that," she soothed. "The letter was so well done. I know. But it's a fake, just the same. Grandy, what I can't understand is, what's he doing all this for? And what shall we do? You'll throw him out, won't you?"

Grandy said nothing.

"What do you think?" she cried.

"Oh, poor child," he said. "I was thinking what a dreadful day you've had. Poor darling, it's a wonder you didn't begin to think you were out of your mind."

"I pretty near did," she confessed.

"It was wicked."

"Yes, it was," she agreed, her eyes smarting with a rush of self-pity. "You don't know how confusing it was. I had to keep telling myself to hold everything and wait, because you'd fix him! And you will, won't you, Grandy?"

"Oh, yes, I'll fix him," said Grandy. She made a little satisfied sigh. "You see, duck, we did feel so dreadfully sad. And he seemed to feel the same. Quite as if he'd known you. I want you to understand—"

"Darling, I don't blame you."

"But I blame myself," said Grandy. "To think we pitied him and let him stay! Of course, he must have supposed you would never turn up."

"He thought I was dead. He thought I'd never come back to tell you he was lying." She nodded.

"We must ask ourselves," said Grandy, "what he wants here."

A car roared out the drive and off down the road. Grandy's pince-nez fell and dangled on the cord. "Dear me, what was that?"

"A car," said Mathilda impatiently. "Grandy, what is it about Althea? Why did they go off together?"

Grandy said, almost absent-mindedly, "You see, Tyl, Francis told me that you couldn't remember him."

She was amazed. "He told you? When?"

"As soon as you came. While you were upstairs."

"Before dinner?" her voice squeaked.

"Yes, right away."

"Then— Oh, Grandy, you guessed it was all a lie. You did know."

"Why, yes. I knew."

Mathilda sank back, puzzled, bothered.

"What I assumed was that his disappearing with Althea was a part of his act," said Grandy, shifting in the chair. "He was your poor, flouted, forgotten lover, and of course he had to be comforted. Althea's done a good deal of that sort of thing," he mused—"comforting Francis."

"I imagine," said Tyl faintly. She thought, *Althea would.* Faint color came to her face.

"Althea's impulse was to be kind," said Grandy, "and it was kind."

She thought, *But Althea's impulse isn't to be kind. That's not so.* She said, "Jane has impulses too. She climbed out her window just now to meet him in the garden."

"Eh?"

"Oh, yes, I saw them."

"Jane?"

Mathilda nodded. She thought, *How many women does he need to comfort him*? Her cheeks were hot. "More part of his act," she said.

"But what's the act designed for, eh, Tyl?" Grandy looked both shrewd and stern. "I think we must know that. We must find out. Yes. You see, I told Francis we'd—er—wait."

"Wait?" Mathilda looked at him, surprised. "Wait?" she cried again, indignantly. Yet she wasn't as indignant as she might have been.

Grandy said, "Because I wonder what he's after, and I'd like to know. Yes. I'd like very much to know."

"So would I." Mathilda felt a little flustered, a little lost.

"You see, duck"—Grandy leaned toward her; his voice took on its old persuasive richness—"the thing's so delicate. We don't want it to be spread around. What fun the newspapers would have if you swear one thing and he continues to swear another. And to do with love and marriage. Oh, Tyl." She looked at him doubtfully. "And yet"—he changed his voice, watching her face—"I should adore to kick him out of here very fast and very hard in a spot where a kick would take the best effect, eh? Perhaps we will do just that Yes, I think so." Then he said crossly, "What does the fellow want? Did he say anything at all, duck? Any little thing?"

She shook her head. "I haven't the slightest idea," she said. "At first I thought he must have wanted to get in here to get close to you. Because he wanted something from you, Grandy. But I—" She shook her head again. She remembered Francis had said he was jealous. "I don't think so any more. I just don't know."

"A very mysterious article, our Francis," mused Grandy. "Now, what could he want of me?"

Mathilda moved her hands, pulling her robe together nervously. Tomorrow they would kick him out like a dog, and he would deserve it. She lifted her chin. Serve him right. She said aloud, "Maybe you're right."

"Eh?"

"Maybe, if we waited, we could find out what he's after," she said weakly. She thought, *What am I saying this for?*

"Let us go slowly," said Grandy thoughtfully. She had a sensation of relief. They both relaxed, as if a decision had been taken. But Grandy had another thought. "Naturally, duck, you dislike him. I could see, at the table—"

"Naturally," she said.

"Therefore, if he annoys you in any way, if even his being here or anything he does—"

Mathilda tossed her head. She thought, *I won't let myself be annoyed.*

Grandy said, with sudden, almost boyish pleasure, "But isn't it the damnedest thing!" and Mathilda looked at his twinkling black eyes and she laughed.

"It certainly is," she agreed. "Oh, Grandy, I feel so much better now."

"Don't you let him make you think you've had amnesia," scolded Grandy fondly. "Don't you let him shake you, duck. Or undermine your confidence. No. He shan't do that. Not if I know it!"

Grandy kissed her. He went out. The door fell softly closed. She stood quite still a moment. *It's all right. It's all right. Of course, it's all right.* She slipped off the rosy robe. *Grandy believes me.* Mathilda brushed her teeth very thoroughly and vigorously. She put herself to bed with great decision and firmness. It was almost as if she had to prove she was firm and unshaken.

Grandy's beautiful bathroom, a bubble of glass and luxury, had been designed and built for him by one of his famous friends, an architect of the modern school. It had been installed for some four years. Before that, Grandy had for his own the bath between his room and the garden room, which bath now served the garden room alone. The connecting door to Grandy's room had been locked and forgotten.

So it was that Jane, sitting in the dark with her eye to the faintest crack at the edge of her own door, where she had just not quite closed it, saw Grandy come out of Mathilda's room, the gray room, cross the hall and pass Althea's door without a glance. She saw him go up toward the front of the house and enter his own place. She did not see him come out again, as indeed he did not, for she watched until dawn.

But Althea, gargling her throat, heard his tapping on the locked and bolted door.

"Grandy?"

"Slip the latch, chickabiddy. Are you decent?"

Althea slipped the latch. "I'm decent," she said sulkily.

He stood in the half-open door, looking at her with a worried frown. "Oliver?"

"Oh." Althea slashed at the rack with her towel. She had a white satin negligee pulled tight around her hips. The wide sleeves were embroidered in silver. "We had a fight. A regular knock-down, drag-out."

"I'm so sorry," said Grandy. "So sorry, dear."

"He'll get over it," she said. She looked angry to the point of tears.

"Was it because of Francis?"

"Such stupid nonsense!" cried Althea.

"He thought—"

"I don't know what he thought, but I can guess. Just because I wouldn't tell him what we were talking about"

"But why not, chicken?" Grandy moved in a little, all benevolence, all loving concern.

"I might have told him if he hadn't been so nasty." She sniffed. "Oliver gets on a high horse and he's just unbearable."

"Then it wasn't a secret?"

"I don't know," she said thoughtfully. A funny cruel little smile grew on her sulky face. "You know, Tyl's a sly one."

"Tyl?" Grandy showed his innocent surprise.

"Francis didn't tell me much," she said, "but he's all upset." She turned away to reach for her lotion. Grandy didn't move. "Such a lot of jealous nonsense!" she stormed. "So Oliver's gone off for the night, and let him! It'll do him good! After all, if Francis wanted me to talk to him, why shouldn't I? Francis isn't very happy."

"Why shouldn't you, indeed?" murmured Grandy mildly. "But you're upset now, chickabiddy, and you mustn't be. It spoils your pretty face."

Althea looked into the mirror.

"Better sleep," said Grandy gently. "Better try to sleep it all away."

"I know," she said. She turned to him repentantly. "Oh, Grandy, you're such a sweet—"

"I want you to sleep well," he said, petting her. One hand on her silver hair, he reached in his pocket with the other. "Some of your little pills, darling? They'll help you."

"Yes," she said. "Grandy, sometimes Oliver's so stupid."

"There," he said. "There. There are these little adjustments."

She took the pills childishly, a lot of them. He held the glass of water for her. She turned to dry her lips. "I hope I don't dream."

Grandy went around the sides of the glass with a towel slowly. He put the glass in her hand. Automatically, she set it in its place.

"Latch the door, chickabiddy. Sleep well." His beaked, beaming face, alight with loving-kindness, remained in the door a brief moment.

"You, too, Grandy," said Althea affectionately. She flicked the latch.

Grandy slept well enough. Jane's head ached where she rested it against her door. Francis, in the garden, was cold. Mathilda had dreams. Oliver, down at the country club, couldn't sleep at all. Althea slept and dreamed no more.

17

THE SUDDEN and unexpected death of Althea Conover Keane, caused by an overdose of sleeping tablets, was called an accident. Tom Gahagen was handling the case himself. He had them all together in Grandy's study, late that morning. All, that is, but Jane Moynihan, who had gone off to New York early. She had been on her train before Oliver came home. It was, of course, Oliver who came home in the morning and, finding it impossible to waken his wife by pounding on the locked bedroom door, had got in through a window finally, and found what there was of her.

Grandy sat behind his desk, and Mathilda's heart ached for him as, indeed, it also ached for poor white-faced Oliver for poor Althea, for the dreary day, for herself, for everything. Grandy's hands shaded his face and he kept looking down at the polished wood, too desperately sad to raise his eyes, even to answer questions.

In this privacy, Gahagen at first said he assumed it was suicide. There was the fact that she had locked herself in, locked the hall door after Oliver when he had left her, about midnight. The connecting bathroom door to Grandy's room was bolted, and had been for years. She was securely locked in. She had wanted to be alone. The stuff she had taken was available there in her medicine cabinet. Althea had been fond of dosing herself. Locked in alone, obviously she took the stuff herself.

Added to this was her note. "Darling. Forgive me, please do," it read, and it was signed boldly with her big sprawling "Althea," of which the last two letters trailed off insolently, as if she assumed it wasn't necessary to be legible. Everyone would know.

A sad and cryptic little note, it was. Francis had found it on the floor, after Oliver had got in through the window and cried out and opened the door, and Grandy had rushed in to stand by the bed and look down at her. In all the confusion, Francis had seen the paper fluttering at Grandy's slippered feet, stirred, no doubt, by the breeze of his passing.

"Now, I'm mighty sorry," Gahagen said, "but I've got to ask you if anybody knows why she'd have wanted to do a thing like this?" The silence fell in a chunk, as it did here, in this unnaturally soundproofed atmosphere. "What did she mean— 'Forgive me'?"

Tyl thought, *But that was what she always said*. She remembered Althea's easy, charming "Forgive me's." Something she, herself, could not say at all. The phrase sounded to Tyl, in her own mouth, pretentious and wrong. For Althea it had been so easy. "Forgive me for not telephoning yesterday." "Forgive me for splashing your dress." "Forgive me for not listening." Gahagen wouldn't know how trivial a matter could call out that phrase. She felt too heavy to make the effort to tell him so.

"Who's the note meant for?" he was insisting. "Who's 'darling'?"

Oh, anybody, thought Tyl. *Everybody*.

Grandy answered as if he tolled a bell. "Surely she meant 'Forgive me for what I am about to do.' God help me, I was afraid."

"Afraid?"

"I don't like to say this now. Yet it's all I can think of. It obsesses me. I had a warning."

"What do you mean, Luther?"

"Premonition. The house felt wrong. She was not right. Not herself." Grandy took off his pince-nez and rubbed his nose. The homely gesture punctuated his talk. It was as if he'd made a homely gesture to reassure himself.

"Was it something she said, Luther?"

"No, nothing she said. Nothing she did. Nothing I can describe. It was . . . the lurking death wish that lies so secretly in the heart. . . . Oh, my house," groaned Grandy, "my poor tragic house." Tyl felt the world would come apart at the seams.

"Sorry, Luther," said Tom Gahagen. "You know I'm sorry. Got to ask a few questions, get it straightened out." He shifted uneasily.

Grandy said, "Don't mind me, Tom." Then, in tones of pure heartbreak, "I am wondering, of course, what I ought to have done that I left undone."

"Aren't we all?" said Francis in a queer, harsh, angry voice. It was as if he'd been rude. Grandy's gentleness reproached him.

Oliver said monotonously, "We had a quarrel, a dumb, jealous quarrel. She'd been out in the guest house with Howard, and I didn't like it. So we said a lot of bitter, nasty stuff and I slammed out of here. She wouldn't tell me what they'd talked about, and I wanted to know. I thought it was my business. She said it wasn't." The careful voice broke. "It couldn't have been over me that she did it. Because I didn't matter that much to Althea, and that's the truth."

It didn't sound like Oliver. He'd been shocked into honest humility. Tyl could have wept for him.

Gahagen looked at Francis. "What were you and Mrs. Keane talking about so long?" he asked with cold precision.

Francis said, "She was in no suicidal mood."

"What d'you mean?"

"She was in no suicidal mood." He repeated his statement quietly. "I spent a good while last evening talking to her, and I would have known."

"What were you talking about?"

Francis shrugged. "As a matter of fact, I was telling her my troubles, and she was very kind," he said smoothly. "And she was not thinking about suicide."

Gahagen's glance passed from one young man to the other. His thought was transparent on his tight face. A triangle. Jealousy. Trouble. No way to get to the bottom of it.

Grandy said softly, "We can't be sure that note was not just a note she'd written some other time. Perhaps this was an accident. . . . Is that possible, Tom?"

Gahagen examined this soft suggestion and thought he understood it. Some tangle of emotions here that could not be publicly explained.

Mathilda spoke up at last. "Althea did use that phrase, 'Forgive me,' such a lot."

"She did. She did," murmured Grandy. "You're right, Tyl. So she did."

"You don't think it was a suicide note at all?" Gahagen sounded tentative, as if he might, in the end, take their word for it.

Grandy said, "Not necessarily. Quite possibly, it wasn't."

Francis said coldly—almost as if he knew, Tyl thought—"She didn't commit suicide, Mr. Gahagen."

"Then you think it was an accident?"

Francis didn't answer.

But Oliver's new and bitter voice said without drama, "I'd rather think so."

There was one of those silences.

"She was," said Francis firmly, insistently, even loudly, "in no more suicidal mood than Mathilda is right now."

Heads turned. What an odd thing to say! Gahagen's brows made puzzled motions.

"I'd like you all to look at Mathilda," said Francis easily. That is, his voice was easy; his arm, hanging over the back of the chair he sat in, was dangling with an effect of being relaxed. But here were two hard little lines near his mouth that Jane would have recognized.

"Why should we look at Mathilda?" purred Grandy. He had himself looked up at last. His black eyes were narrow behind his glasses. He looked wary and alert and as if he were listening hard, trying to hear more than Francis' quiet voice as it went on.

"Because I don't care for these suicidal rumors," said Francis. "I don't like premonitions after the fact. I want all of you to look very carefully at Mathilda, and if you see anything . . . ominous, then let us arrange to take very good care of her." Francis opened his hand, looked at the palm, turned it over, let it fall. "Since two pretty young girls have died in this house," he said, "I'd just as soon there wasn't any third one. So take a good look at Mathilda now. And if she's in a dangerous mood, let's have nurses in and watch her. Let's take no more chances."

There was silence—rather a strained silence. Tyl shook her head. "I don't understand."

"You want to live, don't you? You're not depressed? Not brooding? Not low? You feel well? You're young and looking forward? You've got something to live for?" Francis barked questions at her harshly, angrily. "You don't want to die?"

"Of course I don't want to die! I don't know what you're talking about!" She was so angry she stood up without knowing she had done so. With her head thrown back, her chin up, eyes bright, her breath drawn with indignation, her lovely figure taut and poised, she was most vividly alive.

"Now, Mrs. Howard—" Gahagen began soothingly.

Mathilda flashed around to face him. She would have said she was not Mrs. Howard, but Grandy was around his desk and beside her suddenly, and his hands on her shoulders were quieting and warning her. "There, duckling, there. Francis worries. Naturally. Naturally. You mustn't be angry." He turned to Gahagen. "I think he's made a point," he said. "We could not possibly say there was any mood at all. I can't condemn—" Grandy's voice broke a little. "I dare not damn Althea with a piece of imagined nonsense which may have been my own mood after all. And if we can't say for sure, Tom, ought we not to say it was an accident?"

"That—er—note—" began the detective.

"Such a strange little note," said Grandy. "So vague. So meaningless. I fancy she's written such a note to me or Oliver many a time. And as long as we do not know her reasons or even whether she had any, need we mention any note? To—to people? Frankly, Tom"—Grandy compressed his lips—"I don't want to hear them speculating. I don't want to hear their guesses. I don't want to know they're wondering why Althea wanted to die. For myself, I would rather believe Althea left us accidentally. I do earnestly believe that she loved and trusted us enough to wish to stay."

Francis put both hands over his face.

Tyl thought, *Francis is more upset than Oliver, even.* She thought, *Poor Althea, how could she make a mistake and die*? She thought, *Oh, my poor Grandy!* Pity and grief wheeled around, tumbled each other in her consciousness and yet hardly roused her. They were pale images of coming emotions, only their mental shadows.

But Francis' hands were hiding a black and deadly anger, full grown.

18

All afternoon people came. Tyl was still encased in an aching paralysis that hadn't yet sharpened to pain. It didn't occur to her not to remain in the long room, not to stay there and bear it. She was there, and people came—Grandy's friends—and she stayed and watched and listened numbly.

Grandy was in his big chair. No tears, no sighs, no break in the rich gentleness of his voice. He made kind little inquiries of his friends about their daily affairs. Ever so gently, he kept his grief private. The assumption was that it lay too deep for tears. Tyl saw more than one turn away from him with a convulsed face. It was so beautiful a performance, such a touching thing.

Grandy's friends. Personalities, all of them. They would go to him and receive his gentle greeting, his sweet questions. Then they would go to Oliver, who was in the room, although he seemed not to know where he was exactly, and only stammered "Oh, hello," and "Thanks" and "Yes" or "No," stupidly. Then they would come to Tyl and Francis, who was there beside her, and they would congratulate her, weakly, on being alive. They muted their joy in her return in deference to the death in the house. It was as if they were all saying, "Too bad. He's lost his beauty, though of course he's got this one back. Too bad."

Althea would be a legend. The lovely girl with the silver eyes who died so young. *She'll never grow old*, Tyl thought, *but stay young and lovely in their memories. They will forgive her for everything. Well*, she thought, *I forgive her*.

Francis was introduced as Mathilda's husband. It didn't seem to matter. It was too hard to explain now. Too involved and fantastic. Let it go.

Francis was taking a good deal on himself. It was he who, when the emotional pressure got too high, knew how to break the fever. When Schmedlinova made a gliding run all the way down to Grandy, wailing like a Russian banshee, it was Francis who made a cynical aside and steadied Mathilda's jumping heart. It was Francis who was at her elbow to say the right thing when she couldn't think of what to say at all. She found her eyes meeting his over people's heads. They seemed to have suddenly acquired a full code of signals that went easily between them. It was he who rescued Oliver from the poet who kept quoting, when Mathilda asked him to with her eyebrow. He took slobbering old Mrs. Campbell away before Mathilda screamed. It was his shoulder she found behind her when a sudden wave of fatigue sent her reeling backward. It was Francis who told her quite rudely, at six o'clock, to go upstairs and lie down. It was Francis who brought her a tray, who pulled the comforter over her feet, who dimmed the light. Lying on her bed, weary and numb, she supposed, with dull surprise, that Francis had been acting very like a husband.

When Jane got off the train at seven-thirty, Gahagen's men were there to meet her. They took her to his office without telling her why. It was obvious that she hadn't known what had happened to Althea. She nearly fainted when they told her. In fact, Gahagen was alarmed and called the doctor. The girl was badly shocked. It was no fake, either. Gahagen was sorry that his duty had led him to distress her. After all, the poor little kid didn't know anything, had nothing to tell them, sat there twisting her hands, looked dazed and unhappy. Gahagen sent a man to run her up to Grandy's house.

Francis had taken so much on himself that it was only natural for him to meet her at the door and put his arm around her.

What they exchanged under their breaths was not much, because Grandy's voice said, "Is that Jane?" and people leaned around the arch to say that Grandy was asking for her. It was only natural that Francis should keep his arm around her and lead her to Grandy's throne.

It was a lovely scene. The yellow-haired child in the powder-blue suit with the little white collar kneeling there. Dear old Grandy bent over her so tenderly. And that tall, good-looking Howard man, standing there with Jane's little blue cap in his hand, that he'd picked up when it fell. The long room was quiet.

"I know," Grandy said. "I know, child. I know." His voice was soft and sympathetic, and it didn't change as it went on to ask, "What were you doing in the garden last night with Francis?"

Jane cut a sob in two. Francis, standing by, looked perfectly blank. He felt himself to be within the range of Grandy's eyes, although those eyes were kept on Jane. He struggled for blankness.

Jane took down the handkerchief, revealed her tousled face, all lumpy with weeping. "Oh, Mr. Grandison, I didn't know you knew. I'm sorry."

"Sorry about what, dear?" They were speaking low. The people in the room couldn't hear what they were saying. It all went for part of the tender little scene.

"He only had an hour," wept Jane. "It wasn't anybody's fault I told him he shouldn't have come and tried to see me, but, seeing that he had, I couldn't just tell him to go away. So I thought it wouldn't really . . . disturb you."

Grandy said, "You're telling me it wasn't Francis?"

"Oh, no," said Jane. "Of course it wasn't. It was a—a boy I know. I'll never do it again, sir. I'm so sorry."

Grandy said, "But, my dear, I was not complaining. I was curious, y'know. Next time bring him indoors, child. We are not ogres."

Jane began to cry again, as if such kindness were too much to bear.

Francis said, "What's this about? Something to do with me?"

"Tyl thought she . . . saw you," Grandy said, with a curious little break of hesitation and doubt. His eyes turned. Not his head.

"Tyl did?" said Francis. He kept his face blank, turned his eyes, not his head. Too bad. Tough on Mathilda, but the kid would have to put up with this. It looked as if Jane had really fooled him. But at any rate, Tyl's evidence on what she knew or saw was tending to seem more and more unreliable.

Jane was getting to her feet. Francis took her arm. He said kindly, with just a trace of absent-mindedness, "Hadn't you better come along upstairs and wash your face or something?"

In her room they faced each other. "Well?"

She said, "I got it."

"What we thought?"

"Yes." She told him rapidly and rather mechanically. "I listened to it myself. Told them a wild story about a bet. I got a girl there to listen with me, as a witness. Got it cold, and it's what we want. The Phantom Chief said 'Burn tenderly' only once in that record, and he said it at ten-thirty-five."

"Fifteen minutes." Francis struck his palm with his other fist.

"Yes," said Jane. There was no triumph.

"And Rosaleen hanging since the fuse blew at ten-twenty. That's proof."

"Yes," said Jane.

"Proof!" Francis was bitter and old again. "Jane, he's the devil.

How can we fight the devil? That tongue of his, the power of it! He molds the thoughts in people's heads with his tongue, Jane. Their brains melt. He makes them think what he wants them to think. They're all his puppets. And he's the great director. Look at him now. He's killed twice, committed two murders, and everybody is down there weeping for him."

"Did he . . . kill Althea too?"

"Of course he killed Althea!" swore Francis.

"I couldn't tell Gahagen this alone, but now—"

"Oh, yes, we will now take our nice neat proof to the police," said Francis. "What proof?"

"The time, the radio, the record—all of it. . . . Fran, what's the matter?"

"I can swear Althea told me what she heard on the radio and when she heard it. But you realize . . . Althea isn't here any more."

"You mean we can't—oh, Fran—can't prove it?"

"If I had another witness—"

"Lie then," said Jane fiercely. "I'll say I heard her tell you."

"When?"

"Any time you say."

"You were in the house with them."

"Then you'll have to say she told you some other time."

"When?"

"Oh, I don't know."

"Not you, Jane. Not you, anyhow. It's too dangerous. Maybe you fooled them. All the more reason to keep you out of it now."

"But I'm not out. Why is it any more dangerous?"

"For God's sake, anything's dangerous, anything near him! It's dangerous for us to stand here and talk. It's dangerous to look sidewise at him. I stuck my neck out this morning. Maybe he'll chop my head off before dawn."

"Fran!"

"Why not? He must be on the track of why I'm hanging around here. He must know by now. He's too smart not to see my motive sticking out like a sore thumb. Oh, he's caught on. I hope he hasn't caught on to you. He's quick too. No sooner did he realize that the police knew a fuse had blown . . . Althea's snuffed out. Quick. Neat. No fuss, no bother. Althea was quietly assisted to her grave, all right. And no nasty little loose ends this time, either."

"But you think—you're sure he did it?"

"He did it." Francis dropped his hands. His voice was sick. "But I can't prove it. There's no proof at all. And if he knows now what I'm after, I expect he'll arrange to deal with me."

"You're different," said Jane sharply. "You're no girl."

"True," said Francis. "True. Just the same, if anything does go wrong—"

"Oh, Fran!" Jane shivered.

"Remember Grandy's back-door caller?"

"Do you mean Press, the garbage man?"

"Yes."

"Why?"

"Because," said Francis thoughtfully, "he comes to the back door. And I'm young and strong."

"I'll remember," said Jane. "But what are you going to do?"

"See here. No matter what happens, don't let anything make you admit you're . . . on my side. Mind that, Jane. Promise. Never mind, I've got a better idea. You go home. Resign. Nobody would blame you."

"But what are you going to do?"

"I'll try a bluff."

"What do you mean?"

"I'll insist I've got a witness to what Althea told me. I'll spread out the whole case against him. Pretend it's complete. Maybe I can bluff him. I've got to try. If I could only catch him off guard. Let him make one slip of that tongue! Don't you see, Jane, it could add just enough— You be in there and we—" He broke off.

"I'm not going home," said Jane. "You see, you need me."

"But how am I going to protect you? How can I protect Mathilda?"

"Mathilda?"

He was impatient. Couldn't she see Mathilda was in the most dreadful danger? Couldn't she realize, as he did so clearly, that some one of these days that proud head, those long lovely legs, the exciting green eyes, the whole lovely, bewildered girl, could die? If the old man took a notion—

"Yes, damn it, of course!" he cried. "Look, he's got to get rid of her someday. How am I going to be sure she's safe? She thinks the world of him. She'd do anything he asked, any time. Won't stop to think, because she's clinging to him now. Because she's got to believe in something! And, dear God, how can she believe in me? It's driving me"—he calmed down—"a bit wild," he confessed.

"But he wouldn't dare!"

"Jane, he's more dangerous than you know. He's what Rosaleen said. Perfectly selfish. There's nothing to make him hesitate."

"Can't we go to the police now?"

"Yes, try it. Maybe Gahagen will listen. I wish we had the cold proof. Jane, Grandy'll talk himself out of what we've got. My word's going to be less than enough, after the lies I've told. I don't see how Gahagen can listen."

Jane looked at his face and nearly wept.

"Unless— After all, he's guilty," said Francis. "And he's got guilt in his mind and a mixture of lies and truth to remember. He could slip. It's the only thing I can see to try. Attack. With all I've got. Bluff him down. So," he said rather softly, "I'll try . . . one more legal way."

"What do you mean?"

"Maybe you'll have to go outside the law to get the devil."

"Fran!"

"Sh-h."

Grandy was coming up the stairs. They slipped Jane's door tightly shut and stood without breathing.

If he was coming in here— If he were to find them whispering together—

Luther Grandison was near a violent death just then, as he walked placidly past the door where it was waiting and went into Mathilda's room instead.

19

Nor did he know that Francis went like a cat out Jane's window to the kitchen-porch roof and that he clung, tooth and nail, in the angle the house made there outside Mathilda's window or that he watched, one foot on the sill, cheek on the house wall, fingers wound in a vine. Grandy didn't know. Francis couldn't hear. Through the glass he tried to read across the dim room those thin, mobile lips through which the voice was pouring.

"Resting, darling?"

"I'm awake."

"Poor Tyl. Poor sweet Tyl."

"Oh, Grandy."

"Hush, don't cry." Grandy sat down, heavy and sad. "You're all right, Tyl?"

His anxiety pricked her like the tip of a knife he was trying out. "Of course," she said.

"Because it frightens me. I'm afraid."

"Don't be afraid, Grandy. I'm all right." She sat up. "You're thinking of what Francis said this morning?"

"I can't help thinking. There's that old, old, ancient rule of three. It frightens me."

Tyl's pulse began to pound in her throat.

"Make me a promise, sweetheart," Grandy said.

"Of course."

"Promise you'll come straight to me if you feel—if you have any feelings at all that you can't cope with or bear. Promise, Tyl?"

"Yes, Grandy."

"There's a pressure in my house. You can't see it, of course. You can't hear it. Five senses don't betray it to you, but you feel it all the same. I was afraid of it before. It's death, I think. Not our familiar death that comes on schedule for the old or the sick. This is Death, the fascinator. The Death that's like a dark lover. Don't you see, duck? If it got Althea, it was because it got her unaware. She didn't know. She hadn't been warned. There's an attraction, a dreadful pull. Have you never stood on the edge of a steep drop, Tyl, and felt the urge to go over?"

"Yes," she whispered. "Yes, Grandy."

"It's similar, similar. Pressure. Pull. What difference? Something wants you to go over and be done with everything. Francis was so right, duckling, to be afraid."

Tyl tightened her hands on the coverlet. She had been lying on top of the bed, still dressed. Now she sat up, tense, not resting her back against the headboard. The light was dim. Grandy's face was in darkness. His voice was vibrant. She could feel the vibrations in her breast.

"You mustn't worry about me," she said as stoutly as she could. "Please, Grandy. I do love you so. And I'm all right"

"Bless you."

"Grandy," she whispered, "if you're frightened, it scares me more than anything. Don't talk any more. Not about that."

She reached across. She thought he glanced at her, although she couldn't be sure, since his head didn't move in the dusk. Her fingers found the chain and she pulled on her light near the bed. "Let's talk about something else." She sent her voice high and gay.

"Please, Grandy. Darling, I brought you a present and you haven't even seen it. I nearly forgot."

It took all the strength she had to be so gay. It took all the courage she could find to try to change the mood for him, as he had so often done for her.

"A present?" he said. His effort was obvious. But he understood and he would play. He would try to be cheerful. "A present for me!"

She slid off the bed and ran to her dresser. The bag of Dutch chocolates was in the drawer. Grandy took it in his hands. He bowed his head. For a dreadful moment she thought he was going to weep. But he did not. He opened the bag gleefully. He took a handful out and tossed them gaily on the bed. For her, he said. Their secret. Their childish secret hoard of goodies. He made a show of it. It should have been such fun.

But all the time she could hear the tears unshed behind his laughter, and when, at last, he kissed her gently on the cheek, and when he went away, clutching the bag of chocolates to his heart, Tyl threw herself on the bed and burst into tearing sobs.

Dear, dearest Grandy, he'd tried so hard, but it was enough to break your heart to see how hard he had to try.

20

HER EARS muffled by the sounds of her own weeping, it was a while before she heard the staccato tapping on the glass. Mathilda sat up, face wet, eyes red, hair tousled, frozen in the very image of distress, all rumpled by it. She saw him clinging there outside her window.

She knew who it was, and in a curious mood of suspended emotion she got off the bed and went calmly to open the window. Francis scrambled in. He gave her a quick look, enigmatic, and went immediately to lock the door to the hall. Tyl opened her mouth to protest. He hushed her.

"What was Grandy saying?"

She looked dumbly at him, the tears drying on her cheeks. For the moment, she couldn't remember what it was Grandy had been saying. Francis' face was serious, but his eyes hadn't that dark, reproachful, tortured look. On the contrary, they looked down at her with a warm light behind them, something simpler and more friendly than love.

He said, "I do wish you could trust me, Mathilda. I wish you could trust me a little bit, anyhow. I don't know what I'm going to do about you."

"You needn't do anything about me, thank you!" she said fiercely.

His hand on her arm invited her to sit down on the bed. He pulled the dressing-table bench over. They sat there, knee to knee. It seemed absurd, yet Mathilda had a feeling, half memory, that she owed him some courtesy. She sat where he had put her, and prepared to listen.

"You haven't believed very much of what I've told you," he asked her gently, "have you, Mathilda?"

"No."

"There's one thing maybe you could believe, if you'd try. I don't want anything bad to happen to you."

"Why does everybody think something bad might h-happen?" Her voice shook. "I'm all right."

He took her hands suddenly and eagerly. "What did he say? He was talking to you about something happening, was he?" She didn't answer. Francis released her hands, although she hadn't tried to pull away. "I wish you could believe me. This is the damnedest mess. I know. You've got good reasons not to trust me an inch. And yet—Mathilda, listen. I never did think there was any danger that you'd kill yourself. Can you believe that? I was only trying to fix it so nothing would happen to you."

She shook her head, couldn't understand.

He went on desperately, "Now I'm going to do one thing more . . . might help. I want to ask you— I want to beg you to make it a little easier."

"What do you think might happen to me?" she insisted. Her green eyes challenged.

His dark eyes wavered. Then they came back boldly. "You might as well know that much. I don't want you to be murdered."

"To be what?"

"Murdered, as Rosaleen was. Althea too." His voice was very low. Mathilda drew away, leaned back, away from him, watching his face. He was watching hers. It was a strange duel between them.

"Why do you think they were murdered?" she said at last. "Are you a detective or what?" She was thinking, *This explains*— And yet nothing was quite clear.

"I'm no detective," Francis said. "I'm just a blundering ass, tangled up in a mess here. And one girl died who might have lived if I'd stayed out of it. I don't want you to be another."

"You have been lying," said Mathilda. She sat up straighter. "You admit it now, don't you? All of that stuff in New York, all those people—you lied. You fixed it."

He didn't answer. He kept watching her face.

"If you admit that," she said, "then I just might believe what you say now."

Evading, he said, "Did you tell Grandy about it?"

"Certainly."

"About my lies?"

"Certainly."

"Did he believe you?"

"Of course he did!" She would have risen in her rage and gone away, but he caught at her hand.

"Don't be angry. I asked a question. I just wanted the answer."

"Grandy knows I wouldn't— He knows it couldn't be true that I— He knows—" she sputtered.

"Then why can't you tell me so, without getting so mad about it?"

"You won't admit you're lying!" she cried. "And I know you're lying. Why won't you?"

"Is Grandy quite sure I was lying?"

Mathilda covered her face with both hands. "Please, go away. Get out of my room. What do you want, anyway?"

He said grimly, "I want to fix it so you'll live, baby. I've got here a will you made."

"A will?"

"Will. Last will and testament. I expect it's one of those things you've forgotten. It was made in the three lost days." Francis' voice and manner had changed. He was casual, glib. "Oh, it's legal, all right. The whole thing is in your handwriting. Perfectly good last will and testament. At least plenty good enough to raise an awful stink if you should die."

"If I should—"

"My object is . . . that you don't die. I believe that if I show this little paper in certain places, it will tend to lengthen your life." He looked at her insolently. No, not insolently, but with a reckless look, a gambling look.

She said, "Oh. Now I understand."

"You do?"

"It was the money." She laughed in his face. It pleased her to see his face sobering, losing some of that wild light. "Why I should have been confused by the lie you told about your wealth— What's one more lie to you? You thought I was dead. You thought I'd never come back! You worked out this whole scheme to chisel in."

"Muscle," he corrected. "Muscle in."

"You saw a chance to get your hands on the Frazier fortune! You're so good at forgeries. You really do lie very well."

Francis looked down at her white angry face. "I really don't know whether I can keep you from being murdered," he said with a curious, detached effect. "I'll try."

Mathilda sprang up. "I'm just beginning to wonder," she blazed, "if your scheme doesn't include my murder!" They were eye to eye now in anger.

"In about a minute," said Francis, "I'm going to spank. I tell you you're in danger of your life. I know it. It makes no least difference to me what kind of liar you choose to call me. I'm some kinds of liar, but this kind I'm not. For some strange reason, I don't want you to die."

"Because you love me," sneered Mathilda.

"Unh-uh." It was a negative. It slipped out. It was an admission. She ought to seize upon it triumphantly. But she didn't. "Let's not worry about who loves whom," he went on gently, and he was smiling. "Let's forget that and go back and start over. Do you think you could listen to an idea?"

"What idea?"

"Sh-h, sh-h."

"What idea?" she repeated more quietly.

"I'll show this will to—show this around. Nobody then is going to murder you for your money except me. Right?"

"Right," she said.

"Now we'll protect you from me. Make another will, Mathilda, and hide it. Hide it from me, but tell a stranger where you hide it. The only thing is—promise don't tell—"

"Don't tell whom?"

"Don't tell anyone you know."

Mathilda drew her breath as slowly as she could. She shook herself down to calmness. "You are trying to make me afraid that someone wants to kill me. Why don't you tell me straight out who that person is?"

"Because," said Francis, "there are two Mathildas. One of them could not ever believe me. The other one knows already."

The silence closed in. Suddenly she found herself in Francis' arms. Her impulse was to let go, give up to the warmth there, put her face against him and let the tears through. But she struggled.

"Sorry," he said. He set her back on her own equilibrium. "I know what you're going through. Something about the way you take it breaks my heart." He spoke lightly. His eyes had that warm light. His eyebrows flew up with his smile. He half turned, as if to let her pull herself together. "Lookit! Chocolates!"

She watched him pick up a brightly wrapped candy, peel off the wrapper. She made herself remember that he was a liar. She said, "Your forgeries are so very clever, perhaps I'd better make a genuine will."

She went to her little gray desk, pulled out paper and pen. "To all whom it may concern," she wrote angrily, decisively. She put down the date in big firm figures and underlined it. "This is my will and it supersedes all others, including the one forged by a man who calls himself my husband. I am twenty-two years old, unmarried, perfectly sane. I don't know legal language, but I intend to make my meaning so clear—"

Standing behind her, Francis munched chocolates.

She wrote down that everything she had must belong to her beloved guardian, Luther Grandison. She finished it. She signed it.

Francis nodded. "Good," he said.

She looked up into his eyes. They didn't seem anything but clear and friendly. "If you'll just hide it," he said. "Please, Tyl. And tell a stranger. But only a stranger. What harm can that do? Call it a whim. Call it anything. Give me that little bit of trust or take it for a little bit of advice that can't hurt you."

She thought she could feel the warmth of his presence close above her. The moment crystallized, as some moments will, and for just that while she was aware of the whole setting—herself at the desk with the light falling on her hands, the paper under them, white against the rosy blotter, the green pen lying there. All the background was in her mind, as if she could see it too. The gray walls around them, the furniture, the bed with its yellow spread, its soft pale yellow silken quilt, the hollow in the pillow where her head had been.

And she heard the silence of the house beyond the room's

walls. She was aware of the deserted gardens outside, below, and of the globe of the world turning through the dark toward dawn.

And in the core of the moment was the warmth of his presence, where he stood just behind her, looking down over her shoulder easily, not touching her and yet surrounding her as if there were a shield at her back.

She said, "All right. I'll hide it."

Where had her wrath gone? Where was the stubborn conflict and clash of wills? Mathilda tilted her head, looked up and back. She smiled.

He bent and kissed her warmly, heartily, like a brother, like a friend. An endearing kiss, it asked for nothing. It congratulated her.

Then he put a handful of chocolates in his pocket. "These are good," he said. "Good night." For the second, he hesitated, as if he wondered what to call her. Dear, or what? He touched her shoulder. "Thanks, pal," he said.

Then he put one long leg out the window absurdly, as if he were getting into a pair of trousers. His face grinned at her a last moment over the sill. She heard faint scrambling noises. He was gone.

She put the window down, stepped quickly back and away from it. She didn't want him to see her watching, if he should look back. Because, of course, she wasn't watching.

She had the new will in her hand. She folded it small. She locked about for a place. A little hanging shelf near the bed had some books in it. She took one down, a thin book of poetry—Lucile—in a cardboard case. She put her piece of paper inside, between the book and its case. It wasn't a very good hiding place, but it would do.

Mathilda undressed, got into bed. She told herself that when the light was out she would lie and think things through. She would start at the beginning and be clear about everything. She would try to organize the facts, make some sense out of what had been happening. She would try to understand with her brain, instead of feeling about in the confusion with a straining heart. Instead of drifting in and out of people's arms. She thought, *What a way to behave.* She must—must be clear.

But once the light was off and she lay snug under the yellow comforter, Mathilda fell immediately asleep.

In the morning, she was surprised to find that the door of her room had been locked all night. It wasn't her habit to lock her door. It made her a little ashamed to think she'd forgotten. Because, of course, it was Francis who had locked it, and she'd simply forgotten.

21

GRANDY PUSHED the button; the gadget operated. Francis opened the study door from the living room and came in. He crossed easily to the visitor's chair and sat down. Jane, at her little desk in the corner, kept the rhythm of her typing steady, but the sense of the line she had been typing dissolved into a jumble of meaningless letters, as if she'd suddenly begun to type in code.

Grandy had a cigarette in his holder. He pushed papers fretfully away and leaned on his folded hands. He inquired after Francis' health this morning.

Francis said, "I want to talk to you."

"By all means," said Grandy with some curiosity. . . . "Jane—"

"I'd like Jane to stay, if you don't mind."

"I don't mind." Grandy took the holder out of his mouth and fingered it delicately. He waited.

"Because," said Francis, "I'd like a disinterested person to hear what I am going to say."

"Would you like Jane to take notes?" said Grandy charmingly, obligingly. "She does shorthand very well."

Francis was not diverted. "I came to tell you that you are no longer unsuspected," he said quietly. "And murder's too much, you know, to excuse, even in one who has been so kind."

Grandy's interested expression remained unchanged, unless he looked even more interested. "Please do go on," he said in enchanted tones, as if this were the very thing he had needed to stimulate and excite him.

"When Rosaleen Wright hanged herself that winter morning," said Francis coolly, "she knocked over a lamp, uprooted some wires and blew a fuse."

"So Tom Gahagen was telling me," said Grandy amiably. One would think they approached a puzzle together.

"Your clock on the mantel just beyond that wall was stopped. The time was twenty minutes after ten."

Grandy shifted in his chair. "Yes, yes. All this we know. What's the significance?"

"Althea was in the kitchen that morning?"

"Yes. Certainly. Althea was in the kitchen."

"So were you, Mr. Grandison."

"So was I," he agreed benignly.

"You entered the kitchen," said Francis slowly, "by that door, from this room, at ten thirty-five."

"Whatever makes you think so?"

"You see what it means if that is true?"

Grandy's mouth flattened, expressing distaste. "Something very nasty," he said. "Very nasty." He cocked his head. "Do you follow him, Jane?"

Jane felt a trickle of perspiration down her back. "I don't—no, I don't, sir," she faltered. Her eyes were round as saucers and she looked frightened.

"Really a horrible idea," said Grandy thoughtfully. "That she hanged herself before my eyes, eh? While I watched?"

Francis shrugged.

"Oh, I see!" cried Grandy. "Dear me, I hanged her!"

"The odd part of it is," said Francis, "that you did, and I can prove it."

"That would be very odd indeed," said Grandy. "How?"

"Oh, not the icebox light." Francis tossed this at him. But Grandy's head did not tremble from its bright, interested pose. "Althea told me and one other person, who will remember what was said and so testify." Francis hesitated. "You see you killed Althea a trifle too late."

"So," said Grandy rather more heavily, "Althea too? My lovely girl, the one I've lost."

Jane let out a childish whimper. Grandy looked across at her. "My dear," he said tenderly, "can you bear to hear the rest of this? I'd like you to. Try not to feel. Just listen to the words."

Jane bent her head.

"Now," said Grandy, turning to Francis, his eyes glinting, "proceed, Mr. Howard."

Francis thought, *Jane's fooled him. He's acting for Jane*. He marshaled his attack.

"Althea turned the radio up, if you remember—or even if you don't"—Francis caught and controlled his temper—"at precisely the moment you entered the kitchen and closed that door. She was struck by a phrase said over the air. She remembered it clearly. That program was recorded at the time, Mr. Grandison. It gives away the exact minute. The minute you left this room. And that minute was ten thirty-five. Not earlier."

Grandy said, "My dear boy." He said it gently, with pity. "When did Althea tell you this?"

"The evening—the night she died."

"What a day and a night you've had since." Grandy spoke softly. "That is, if she really did—or even if you, for any reason, believe this story."

Francis found his throat unmanageable. The evil old bird was so full of pity. He was turning it, pretending to be seeing a point of view. He was not worried, not even looking worried. He was not reacting according to plan. The scene wasn't going right. A guilty man, accused, had no business to look so sorry for his accuser, so successfully sorry.

Grandy said, as if to be fair, "After all, you are nearly a stranger here. But even so, dear boy, what reason do you imagine I would have had for such a deed as that?" Then, almost gaily, "Come, Mr. Howard, I must have a motive."

"My wife's money," said Francis, "was and is your motive."

"Eh?"

"You played around with it. Rosaleen Wright found out."

"Oh, dear. Oh, dear." Grandy took off his pince-nez and rubbed his eyes. "Yes?" he said. The black eyes were brimming with mirthful tears. "But Mathilda isn't your wife at all, Mr. Howard. You see, we know that."

Francis heard Jane's gasp. *Oh, good girl, Jane.* He said aloud, coldly, "Would you be willing to let me or anyone examine the records of the Frazier fortune?"

"Certainly," said Grandy. "This does seem so silly. As for Althea's story, what occurs to me, Mr. Howard, is the thought that Althea told no story. I think you invented it."

"Two of us invented it?"

"That's not impossible," said Grandy smoothly. "Who is your—er—corroborator?"

"In view of my opinion of you," said Francis evenly, "I don't believe I care to say."

Grandy leaned back. "You don't mean it," he challenged. "You're not serious."

"I'm serious."

"Isn't it too bad," said Grandy in a moment, "that Althea isn't here to help us? Oh, I see! I see! That's why I'm supposed to have done her in? Well, really, that's not unsound. That's good thriller-level reasoning, Mr. Howard."

Francis bit on his cheek. "Also," he said, struggling to stay calm and seem confident, "there is Rosaleen's false suicide note. Cribbed out of an old book. What did you do? Ask her to copy it one day?"

Grandy's face fell. "Poor Rosaleen. Poor child," he crooned. "I didn't like to point out what she'd done. Poor sick little mind! Did we delve too much, I wonder, into old crimes and ancient madness?"

"Sick mind, my eye!" Francis shot up out of his chair. "And Althea was sick, too, wasn't she? Although nobody saw any signs of it but you. What will Mathilda be when her time comes? Or anybody else you decide to get rid of? Let me show you something now." He slammed the paper down on the desk, keeping his palm on it. "That's Mathilda's will. And I warn you, see to it that Mathilda doesn't die! Because, if she does, I don't think you'll care to have me and my lawyers going into financial history."

Grandy's eyes flickered. Francis held his breath, but the old man's hand was steady. He touched the paper. He read it He took off his pince-nez and looked up.

"A forgery," he said softly. Brown eyes met black. Jane in her corner trembled.

"Do I see it all now?" mused Grandy, cocking his head. "Did you think she was lost at sea? Did you think you'd cut a piece of money with your fantastic story? I can understand so far, yes, indeed. But what are you up to now? Ah! Am I to pay you for suppressing your little ideas?"

Francis could have wrung his skinny neck. Might have done so, indeed, if Jane hadn't cried out.

"There now, you've frightened Jane," said Grandy in pouting reproach. There was no breaking there, no self-betrayal, no guilty squirm, no fear in this man. He was untouched, bland, confident, and the voice was sirup-smooth. Francis knew himself to be too angry to think, to have been outdone in self-control, and out-bluffed.

He turned and said stiffly to Jane, "I'm sorry if I frightened you." He said to Grandy, as quietly as he could, "I'll take my little ideas to Gahagen, then."

"Dear boy," said Grandy warmly, "if you believe all that nonsense, you most certainly should go to Gahagen or someone. Besides," he added ruefully, "although for my part, I only wish I could help you—I'm afraid you do need help rather badly—still, I did rather promise Tyl to kick you out the door."

Francis said, "Don't bother, Mr. Grandison." He left the room.

When he had gone, Jane thought, *For my life, for my life*. She twisted her hands, filled her china-blue eyes with horror. "Oh, Mr. Grandison, wasn't he awful?"

"Poor chap," said Grandy. "The fellow's a fraud, of course. My poor Tyl—"

"Oh, Mr. Grandison!" cried Jane, for her life. "Nobody's going to believe anything he says! He was just trying to make trouble!"

"And well he may make trouble," said Grandy. He put his hands to his forehead wearily. "Run, fetch me some coffee, my dear. That's a good girl. Yes, do."

"Oh, Mr. Grandison!" quavered Jane, still acting for her life. "I can't tell you how sorry I feel that you have to be bothered—"

She got out the door and stood trying to control a fit of nervous shaking.

Grandy drew over his desk phone, gave a number. "Press? . . . Ah, my dear fellow, there is something I'd like you to do for me. . . . Yes, I thought you would." Then his voice cracked like a whip, "This must be quick. Do you understand?"

"Whatever you say," said the man on the other end hopelessly.

22

WHEN MATHILDA got down to the kitchen for her breakfast, there was only Oliver. He was sitting over a saucer full of cigarette butts.

"Where's everybody?" she asked.

"In with Grandy."

"Oh." Mathilda got herself coffee from the stove. She hoped it was good and strong. She had awakened in a cold sweat. She wondered if she was coming down with something. She felt numb and confused and as if a lowering cloud hung over the world, something black and terrifying, ominous, threatening, as if there was worse to come. Perhaps it was only that Althea was dead.

Oliver was lighting another cigarette. He glanced at her nervously as she sat down. "The funeral is this afternoon," he blurted out "They've released the body. Grandy says get it over with."

Mathilda shivered. What could she say? Nothing to say. It was simply stupid to open your mouth and say, "I'm sorry." Oliver put out his cigarette and lit another. He didn't seem to know he was doing so.

"This accident stuff is all right for publication," he blurted, "but it wasn't any accident."

"What do you mean, Oliver?" Tyl put out her hand and touched his. She did feel sorry for him. There must be a way to let him know it.

"Because she must have eaten them! Eaten them!"

"Eaten what?"

"Those pills. By the handful."

"The sleeping dope?"

"Yes, because, listen, Tyl, Doctor Madison knows damn well how she used to love to take a lot of junk. He fixed her up with some extra-mild ones. He told me so, when I worried about it. He knew she'd take too many, too often. He said the effect was mostly psychological, anyhow. Tyl, for her to die, she must have eaten a whole bottle. So she must have wanted to die. Don't you see?"

"I can't believe—"

"You'd better believe it."

"Oliver, you didn't have any stronger pills in there, did you?"

"Never touch the junk. No. Nothing."

Mathilda shook her head. She could feel the cloud, that heavy, depressing, shadowing bulk that seemed to exist in the back of her consciousness, ready to come down and swallow her up in despair. She was afraid. She drank more coffee hastily.

"I can't stop going over that fight we had." Oliver stared at her with reddened eyes. "I can't stop."

"You mustn't do that," said Tyl. She, herself, felt that this was an unsupported statement. If he had asked why not, she couldn't have answered.

"I know," he said. "I know, but I can't stop. 'Burn tenderly.' What does that mean to you?"

"What does what mean?"

"'Burn tenderly.'"

"I don't know. I never heard such a thing."

"Wouldn't you guess it was love stuff? Wouldn't you think it came out of some lousy poem? Or some fancy speech in the movies? 'My heart burns tenderly.'"

"Maybe," she said.

"Yeah."

"What's the matter? Why are you worrying about that?"

Oliver put his head down, and for once his forelock fell over his eyes without the self-conscious boyishness with which he had been known to let it fall. "Althea wouldn't talk that night. Night before last. Not at first. She just wouldn't talk to me at all. But then she laughed and said that out loud. I don't think she meant to, but she said, 'Burn tenderly.' Tyl, I thought she and Francis must have been talking that way—you know, love stuff. Reading each other poems or something. I was mad. I told her what I thought. I said that proved it. She tried to tell me it was something some cook had said on the radio."

"Cook?"

"Yeah. Do you believe it?"

"I don't . . . know."

"I asked her how she'd happened to remember some dumb thing a cook said on the radio, especially at a time like that. She had a story. She said it was because she turned the radio up in the middle of a program. She'd turned it down on account of Grandy coming in, and then she turned it up, and the guy said those two words just out of a clear silence. It sounded funny. She said she'd been telling Francis about it."

"Telling Francis?"

"Do you believe that?"

"It sounds crazy."

"That's what I thought."

"Why should she be telling Francis what some cook said on the radio?"

"Yeah, that's what I wondered. I think—I still think—Oh, I

don't know what I think. Suppose she did carry on with him. Tyl, I'm sorry." His eyes looked desperate. He was lost in this anguish of new honesty.

"That's all right," she said weakly. "Oliver, don't keep beating yourself. She couldn't have been enough involved with Francis to kill herself. Anyhow, Althea wouldn't have killed herself for any such kind of thing. Do you know what I mean?"

Oliver nodded. He seemed to relax a little. "I know," he said. "She was . . . flirtatious, I guess you'd say. She liked to get men interested. That was what interested her. And it would have gone on all our lives."

"I expect it would," said Tyl sadly. It was true. Althea would never want what she had, but would always have watched with her silver eyes for her chance to step in and take what somebody else wanted. It was the act of taking away, the use of her power, that she had savored. Poor, restless, envious, uneasy Althea. Could she have seen herself and, with sudden clarity, known she must never grow old?

"Such a mess," groaned Oliver. "Everything gone wrong. From the minute we married. You got lost. Rosaleen did that . . . thing. Then Francis came, and she— He's very attractive."

"Yes," said Tyl.

"Now, this. I'm talking too much. I'm taking my troubles out on you. Tyl, you're swell. Sometimes I think I played a pretty dirty trick on you too. If I did, I hope you've forgiven me."

"Yes," she said with a shrinking feeling. "Don't talk about it."

"You know, Tyl, your money's a bad thing."

"I know," she whispered.

"I mean"—his eyes begged her to understand—"it works out a way you probably don't realize. Althea was so beautiful, and there was your money, and I kept thinking, 'Am I fooling myself? Is it the money I care for?'"

"I suppose you would," she said painfully.

"It's easy to fool yourself. I've been fooling myself all my life. I don't know how to stop, either."

"Oliver, don't."

"So when Grandy said Althea would never have anything but love to make her happy—"

"Grandy?"

"You see, I didn't notice what was going on. I guess I just couldn't believe that Althea would—well, get interested in me that way. And of course, I didn't know the way you felt, either."

"The way I felt? What way, Oliver?"

"Oh, I mean the way it was. I'm the old-timer around here. You could be sure of me. I mean, you had to be so careful some ordinary fortune hunter didn't try to play up to you. Grandy told me you had a dread of that."

Mathilda hung on to the edge of the table. The cloud was coming down. It was going to get her. She felt sick with fear.

"He cleared that up," Oliver said. "He explained how your love for me was a gentle, friendly feeling, because you felt sure of me on that score. Not real love."

She thought she'd faint. She fought against it.

"Tyl—"

She managed to murmur something. "Everything's been awful this morning. I didn't sleep well." *But I did*, she thought. *I slept too hard and too long.*

"It's been awful. I know." Oliver brooded. "Dear old Grandy, of course, wanted us all to be happy. He was right, wasn't he, about you? I asked you right out that day—you made a wisecrack. I thought—I mean—"

"Don't stammer," she said sharply. "Grandy's always right He knows me better than I know myself, almost."

She thought, *But I mustn't ever tell Grandy how wrong he was or what he did to me. It would break his heart if he knew. Besides, it's all over now, and it doesn't matter. He must have known it wouldn't last. Oh, Grandy must have known. And if I hadn't been so proud and wanted to run away and hide everything, he'd have drawn out the sting long ago. I was a fool. I should have trusted him.* She beat back her depression. She beat back fear.

Then she remembered the strange talk last night with Francis, about the will. The taste of fear rose in her throat. She thought, *What's the matter with me*?

She left Oliver and went toward the living room.

"Don't look like that!" Tyl cried. "Don't!" Jane was in there, crouching against the wall by the study door, like an animal stiff with fear. Tyl's hands went up to her eyes. She thought, *No, I can't stand it.*

"I'm awfully sorry," Jane said, straightening. "I don't know what's the matter with me."

"I'm sorry too," said Mathilda. "I don't know why I . . . screamed at you. I guess it's just nerves." She smiled faintly.

"I guess it's just nerves," Jane agreed. She smiled faintly back.

Tyl thought, watching Jane walk away, *I need another girl to talk to*. It didn't strike her that this was the first time Grandy hadn't seemed better than another girl to talk to.

23

THERE WAS the funeral to face that afternoon. They made themselves sandwiches for lunch and snatched them in the kitchen. It was a queer, unsettled kind of meal, as if they were all just marking time, waiting time out until it should go by and bury Althea and release them to normal processes of grief and adjustment.

Francis wasn't there. The odd thing was that no one mentioned him. Grandy said nothing. Oliver was bound up in his inner struggle and seemed not to notice. It was not Jane's place, perhaps, to say anything about a missing guest. But Mathilda kept expecting him or at least expecting someone to say a word that would explain where he was, where he had gone, for how long. She did not ask any questions herself.

When they set out in the chauffeured car lent by a friend, there were the four of them—Grandy, Oliver, Jane and Mathilda. The four of them got in and settled themselves as if no one were missing. Francis wasn't there.

Mathilda thought perhaps he would meet them at the chapel. He would be among the others and he would come back with them when it was all over. Nobody asked any questions. It was a little strange that Grandy seemed not to have noticed at all. Mathilda's so-called husband was not where he ought to have been, even if he were only pretending. Not there, not by her side. Not there, as he had been yesterday. People would wonder.

Jane was quiet as a mouse. Jane didn't ask. Oliver didn't ask. Mathilda, herself, although the question was beginning to beat hard in her mind, didn't venture to ask. It would have been queer if she were the one to ask. She thought if she waited surely his absence would be explained. If she just waited.

The little chapel downtown in the small city was thronged with friends, the whole picturesque lot of them. Tyl sat beside Grandy and modeled herself after him in frozen calm. *Be a lady. Never betray an emotion.*

The ceremony was only an ordeal. She thought, if only Francis had come. If only he were on her other side, where he ought to be. But that wasn't true. He had no place—no real place and no real obligation. He only pretended. Oh, but why wasn't he there, pretending, now? She counted the scallops in the frieze. This was not the time to feel what you really felt about Althea, or remember her as she was, or try to understand her life and her death. *Don't cry. Count the folds in the curtains. One, two, three, four.*

When it was over, some few friends came back with them and there was tea. Francis wasn't there.

When people had thinned out, drifted off, finally gone, Oliver at last asked the question, "Say, where is Francis? Where's he been? He wasn't there at the chapel, was he?" Oliver's face turned to Mathilda for the answer.

Like throwing a ball, Mathilda thought. *Don't they know!*

"When he left us this morning, I believe be said he was going downtown." Grandy was mildly speculative. "Didn't he, Jane?"

Jane said, "Yes," faintly. "Yes, he did, Mr. Grandison."

"That is strange. . . . Tyl, do you know where Francis is?"

The ball had come back to her. "I don't know where he is," she said stiffly. "I don't know a thing about him. I never did. It's about time all of you knew he isn't my husband."

Jane knew already that Francis was a fraud. That could be seen in the steadiness of her eyes and heard in the murmur she made, which was only polite.

But Oliver was shocked right out of his chair. Mathilda had to tell him the details, and he wanted to hash them over and exclaim and wonder and go around and around over the puzzle of Francis. At the same time, she thought she could see a kind of inner gleam, a repressed sparkle in his eyes when he looked at her. Tyl felt herself getting angry. She answered him in a series of grudging short phrases. She didn't want Oliver's gossipy rehash. She didn't want to hear Oliver's ideas of why people behaved as they did. She didn't want to hear Oliver wondering what made Francis tick. She felt he wouldn't know.

She was sick and ashamed of the emotional background to Francis' story. She couldn't tell them that, of course. How she'd been in such a weeping, wailing, brokenhearted, upset state over Oliver. But without that part the whole story sounded trivial and cold. Here was a man who claimed she had married him. Why had she? Presumably because she had wanted to. And then she forgot. No background of emotional distress to explain how it all might have happened. Her upset and her silly baby thoughts of revenge. Ridiculously, she found herself defending Francis. Of course, it was a lie, but it had been a good lie.

"You don't understand," she cried.

"My God, do you?" cried Oliver, and she was too angry to answer.

Jane said perhaps he'd run away. She said it looking at Grandy as if they two had secrets about Francis.

Mathilda said in anger, "I'm going to bed." How had she got herself into such a temper?

Halfway up the stairs, a ring at the front door stopped her and sent her heart leaping. It was only someone to see Grandy. Might as well go up. But that voice? She stopped and looked down again. All she could see was the top of the man's red head. Francis had dark hair, not quite black. Francis hadn't come back at all; hadn't been seen all day.

24

THE CELLAR was dry. That, at least, was a blessing. He was alive and uninjured. More blessings to count. How long he would be able to count these or to count at all was very doubtful. Francis expected the worst. He expected that an attempt would be made to kill him. He expected it to succeed. He did not know how he could counter such an attempt, bound and tied as he was with strong harsh ropes, gagged as he was with old rags, trussed up like a chicken for the roasting, ridiculously helpless.

It was fantastic to be so helpless. Francis thought of the movies he had seen, of the many, many scenes in which a hero had been marched at the point of a hidden gun out of the cheerful streets to some lonely lair and been tied up. He thought that if he escaped to see another such movie, he would understand, he would sympathize, he would be more anxious. He would not wonder why the fellow went so quietly, nor would he be quite so confident that somehow, with his teeth, or his clever fingers, or by rolling about, the hero would get loose in time.

Francis couldn't see any way to get loose. The ropes were tight and firm. He could barely move his hands. His working fingers grasped at nothing but air or, if he rolled slightly, the bare cement floor of the cellar. The gag was tight too. No use rubbing his cheek against the rough cement. It only scratched and tore his skin. The gag wouldn't move. It was anchored tight. It was all he could do not to choke.

His ankles were bound together. He could not get up, would have had no balance, anyway. And there was nowhere to roll, no advantage to it. This part of the cellar was perfectly empty. The floor, the rough whitewashed walls, a little window high up, one naked light bulb, the wooden door to another room. Nothing else at all.

He had lost track of time. It was night. The little window admitted no daylight any more, although, for a while after he had been brought here, there had been some light, blocked by green bushes, coming dimly through the leaves and the dirt on the glass. Now there was only a black oblong, although some light must come from somewhere—enough to distinguish the white walls from the black window. Just enough for that.

Night would pass. Sooner or later, there would be that dim daylight. It was all he could look forward to, unless the woman should come down with food again. He didn't like to think of that woman. Mrs. Press, he supposed she was. Tall, very thin, emaciated, no more shape than a stick, and no more color. She was a caricature of a woman. A long-jawed face and hair tight back in a bun, all drab, pale gray tones. She looked like a slave, a drudge, one who had been kicked and beaten. She appeared to be perfectly obedient. But what he feared was that she was not obedient, because the eyes in that long, ugly face were neither sad nor dulled. The eyes were full of enthusiasm. He suspected that Mrs. Press would be, if not obedient, rather terrible. He hoped Mr. Press or somebody would be able to keep her in line.

Hope? Well, it sprang eternal, thought Francis. The ache in his arm, where the old wound was, beat with his heart. He began to wonder why he was still alive. He thought he could guess.

At midnight, although Francis didn't know it was only that, he heard them coming down the cellar stairs. Somewhere beyond the wooden door the stairs came down and there was a furnace and such other cellar furniture. Out there he heard their feet and heard their voices. Heard Press say, in his dull voice, "No trouble."

And he heard the rich warm voice of Luther Grandison, the famous voice, so full of sentiment, so beloved on the radio, heard it saying, "Good work, my dear fellow. You were very prompt, and I do appreciate it. Now, let us see."

The wooden door was unbarred from outside. It was opened. Someone turned on the light, and the unshaded bulb blinded him for a moment.

Francis thought, *He'll have to kill me now. He intends to kill me. Or he wouldn't let me see him. He wouldn't come openly.*

Grandy took off his pince-nez delicately. "Ah, yes," he said. "Can you remove that—er—impediment to his speech? I want to talk. You can control him, can't you?"

"Guess so," said Press. He moved indifferently to the business of ungagging his prisoner. He was a strong man, as Francis had discovered before—physically strong. He seemed to have no feeling about what had happened or might happen. Obviously, he carried out orders.

But there was a lean gray shadow behind him, a shadow with gleaming eyes. That woman. Francis knew himself to be afraid.

Press was loosening the gag. As it came off, Francis did choke. He coughed, retched, got control of his breath at last. He said nothing. What was the use, unless he shouted for help, and what was the use of shouting?

Grandy squatted down rather stiffly. After all, he was not young. His fingers fumbled about Francis' body. He was searching for something. He found it and stood again. He had the will in his hands—the will that was supposed to have been written out by Mathilda.

"I think we will just dispose of this," he said distastefully, and lit a match and burned it, holding the paper until the last possible moment, with perfectly steady fingers. Then he dropped the charred ash and stamped on it. The smell of burned paper seemed to fill the place.

Francis thought what a fool he had been. We are so vulnerable to plain, unadorned violence. We tend to think our enemies will play by the rules. We can't conceive of the rules being wiped out. We don't really, except on the battlefield, believe in the existence of ruthless, violent people. We believe them when we see them. He ought to have known better.

He said aloud, "There is a copy."

But Grandy smiled. It was said too late. A copy of a holograph will? Absurd, anyway.

Grandy said, "Now, please. I'll have the name of the person who heard Althea's evidence."

Francis made his mouth say pleasantly, "You will?"

"Oh, yes, I think so," said Grandy, in high spirits. The thin shadow that was Mrs. Press came a little closer. She had something long and sharp in her hand. It was metal. It caught light. Not a knife. An ice pick. Francis began to laugh painfully. It was nearly a giggle. Everything that was happening to him seemed so absurd. Such old stuff. And so effective. It was comical how effective it was, the threat of torture.

Press was leaning indifferently against the wall. Mrs. Press said, "Shall I?"

Grandy was watching Francis with cold speculation. "We'll see," he said.

"It won't be necessary," said Francis. "I'm no hero."

"Very sensible. Go on."

"There was no one," said Francis with perfect truth. "She told me about it down in the guest house that night. We were alone there."

"No second person?" said Grandy softly.

"No one at all."

Grandy lifted an eyebrow. "Mrs. Press," he said.

"No!" cried Francis, outraged. "Don't! I'm telling you the truth! There really isn't— I can't give you a name when there isn't any name."

"Just let us see," said Grandy, nodding. "Life follows bad literature so often, you know. Perhaps he is being a hero. I dare say he wishes to protect that witness."

"There wasn't any witness."

The woman got down on her knees. She put the point of the thing under his thumbnail.

"Who was it?"

"Nobody."

"Who was it?"

"Nobody. I was bluffing."

"What is your name?"

"Francis Howard."

"Not in the mood for the truth yet, Mrs. Press. Continue."

Francis ground his teeth. He mustn't tell his name, because of Jane. Because his name was Jane's name, too, and Grandy must not know. Jane would have the sense to leave his house now. Get out of that house. Jane was so much smarter than she looked. But Mathilda? What could he do for Mathilda? The pain was wicked.

"Sorry!" he gasped. "This is pretty futile! There wasn't anyone! Shall I invent a person?"

Grandy said, "Just one moment, Mrs. Press. . . . Now listen to me. I know your name is not Howard. I understand, now, the trick you played with that marriage license. I realize that you scoured the city and all suburban communities for a bona-fide license issued that day with the name Frazier on it. Finding one for a Mary Frazier was a great stroke of luck. Although you searched for it. You earned it. Of course, it follows that you simply assumed the other name on the license. You had to. I think your first name actually is Francis, all right. Not John. And your surname is not Howard.

"Let me make it plain that I know this because it has been independently checked. A newspaperman actually found the original bride and groom, and interviewed them. He came to me, quite puzzled. Just this evening. I appeared to be puzzled, too, and begged for time, but I was enlightened, you see? Now that you understand how much I know and guess, proceed, Mr. Howard."

Francis thought of his past life. He said, "My name is Shields." It wasn't. He hoped it would pass.

Grandy said, "Thank you. Now, about that witness."

"No witness," said Francis dully. "You can do this forever. I can't stop you." He closed his eyes and waited for the pain. He thought how futile torture really was. There was nothing certain about the results you got, after all. Innocent people would swear to guilt to escape it, as readily as guilty people would give up the truth. There is nothing solid in fear. Nothing a torturer can rely on. Bad evidence, in fact. It ought to be suspect. It almost could not be true. "Can't rely on it," he muttered.

He heard Mrs. Press breathing.

"That will do," said Grandy severely.

Francis felt the moisture form drops on his forehead and begin to roll away.

"I doubt if it matters," said Grandy thoughtfully. "You may have been bluffing. I think we've had enough of this sort of thing." He spoke as if it had all been in rather bad taste.

Mrs. Press said, "A couple of times more—"

"No more," said Grandy.

She obeyed.

Francis opened his eyes and looked curiously at Grandy. "Next?" he inquired.

"My dear boy," said Grandy, as if to say, "Really, need you ask?"

"Am I going to commit suicide? I warn you. I don't think that's altogether a good idea."

"Oh, I agree," said Grandy pleasantly. "It isn't a good idea at all. Jane gave me a thought, you know."

Francis absorbed the shock of her name, prayed it hadn't been noticed.

"Jane suggested to me this evening that perhaps, after your little failure this morning, you had given up your schemes. She wondered if you hadn't simply run away."

Francis tried to look flabbergasted. He thought, *Jane's all right. He's not onto her yet.* He tried to let his battered mouth form a sneer. "That's stupid," he said.

"Not at all," said Grandy brightly. "I think it's perfectly logical. You see, first the scheme to get Mathilda's fortune was spoiled by the fact that Mathilda wasn't dead. The little will, all that careful preparation, wasted. Well, Althea's suicide, so soon after another death of the same kind in my house—of course, it suggested foul play. You would begin to wonder how you could turn that to account. Althea is dead. She can't deny whatever you choose to say she said." Grandy interrupted himself, so abruptly did he change the smooth spinning of a story into accusation. "You found that picture in the paper—the photograph of the clock?"

"Yes," said Francis.

"You pointed it out to Gahagen?"

"Yes."

"Well," said Grandy. "Well, well. Then, even before Althea died, you were scheming. Ah-ha! Perhaps you killed Althea."

Francis said, "I don't have the advantages of two bathrooms."

Grandy said, "Perhaps you put more powerful pills— Dear me, what an alliteration!"

"Planted them?" said Francis helpfully.

"Yes, indeed. You see, it's going to be quite an interesting story."

"I can see that it will be," conceded Francis.

"You have already disappeared. It did look so queer that you weren't at the funeral. It only remains—"

"To dispose of me?"

"Exactly."

Press spoke for the first time. "Look," he said. "Not here."

Francis wanted to whoop with laughter. Was the fellow aroused at last, thinking of his cellar floor?

"Oh, dear me, no. Certainly not here," Grandy reassured him. "My dear fellow, I shouldn't think of it."

"Whatever you say," said Press. He had a bitter, harsh voice. His eyes were without hope and yet smoldering. Francis thought, *He might help me. He's being compelled. None of this is his idea.*

But Press said, "I suppose I've got to do it for you. Only not here," and the flat resignation in his voice was not encouraging.

The woman made a movement. It was as clear as if she'd said it aloud. As if she'd said, "Let me. I'll enjoy it."

"Ah, well, in the eyes of the law we shall be equally responsible," said Grandy cheerfully. "And that, my dear Press, will be pleasant for you. We shall both be of the, unsuspected, eh?" he chuckled. Press simply waited. "Is he perfectly secure here?" asked Grandy. They nodded. "Then I don't think we'll be in any hurry. I must get back. We must think it over, you know. Doubtless, something ingenious will occur to one of us." He turned to leave. His eyes went mockingly to Francis. "You don't ask for your bride?"

Press was putting the gag back into Francis' mouth. It obscured any expression there might have been on Francis' face and prevented him from making an answer.

"I'll take care of Mathilda," said Grandy smoothly, "when the time comes. Let me see—" He had no feeling, no sorrow. The soft regret that purred in his voice was only a habit, a trick in his throat. "You disappear. There will be Jane's story of what you said in my study. Then, of course, Mathilda's story of what you tried to do to her. The marriage hoax. She must tell that to everyone. She will tell it with great indignation. She will tell it so well. Oh, the wickedness of it! What a wicked, wicked fellow you are," crooned Grandy. "But you did not prevail. You were defeated. You ran away." Grandy nodded. "The girls will support me."

Then the wooden door opened, closed. The light went out. Feet traveled toward the steps. Francis listened, hoping it was three pairs of feet. He didn't like the woman.

Yes, he thought, the girls. Mathilda. What Mathilda would tell the police would be only the truth, all the truth she knew. And if Jane tried to tell the truth behind the truth, it would never prevail. Who was Jane to pull down Luther Grandison? She couldn't fight alone. There was no one to help her now.

Mathilda would help destroy herself. She didn't know any better. He understood. She couldn't believe. It was too much to ask of her. Grandy had her in his web, had always had her, and he would keep her and do what he wanted to do, whatever it might be. Spider and fly. Poor courageous little fly. She had courage. She could fight. On the wrong side, but still one could admire. Eyes closed in the dark, he could see her face.

He said under his breath, "Rosaleen, I tried. Listen, little one, I know what he did to you. I tried to punish him."

It seemed to him that Rosaleen forgave him, because he couldn't see her face. It seemed to him that, graciously, her little ghost moved on. He might himself be with her soon, wherever she was. He hoped Grandy's ingenious way would be quick, at least. His hand throbbed and throbbed. The pain was monstrous. It loomed so large in the silent dark.

And leave Mathilda to the mercy of Grandy who had no mercy. Francis thought what he would do if he were loose. And then he tried not to think of such matters. Because he couldn't see any way to get loose. The ropes were still tight and firm. He couldn't move his wrists to speak of. The wounded arm was very weak. The muscles weren't responding. His ankles were numb. Trying to move would rub his skin off, accomplish nothing. The gag was in as firmly as before. He couldn't make a sound. The pounding of his heels on the cement was only a dull thud, could never be heard by the world, if there still was a world up there beyond that black oblong in the wall. Still night. No dawn.

The whole situation was perfectly ridiculous. But ropes are ropes. They held. There was no miracle. Nothing happened during the night to loosen those bonds. When the light began to seep through the green leaves at last and touch the dirty glass, Francis was lying exactly as he had been lying, exactly as helpless, hopeless and lost.

Oh, there was a tiny flicker of hope left, but really it was not sensible. The people going about their business up there in the world would have no suspicion. His helplessness and his plight would be unsuspected. So what he'd tried to do would be of no avail. The best he could do at the time, but it hadn't been good enough. No, no hope. Put it out. And pray for Mathilda. Pray for her.

25

On Friday morning, Grandy's house had fallen into a normal rhythm. Life was going on. It was the reflection of Grandy's own mood, of course. His house and the people in it were susceptible to his moods and always reflected them. And Grandy had taken an interest in breakfast that morning. Grandy had parceled out the household chores in his usual gay fashion. Even Oliver had reached a state of calm and had gone off on errands.

Jane, looking about twelve years old in blue-and-white-checked gingham, was swabbing the floor of Grandy's glittering bathroom. Mathilda herself, in a black skirt and a peasant blouse, was changing linen on the beds. Mirrors reflected them many times.

Mathilda had a prevision of how life, going on, would fill in and smooth over the place where Althea had been. How it would always fill in the empty places, flowing, smoothing, covering. Grandy's house was just the same. Although Althea was gone, Tyl had come back. Rosaleen was gone, but here was Jane. There would always be one girl or another reflected in the mirrors, changing the beds, mopping the floor. The changing of the beds would outlive them all. The little duties, the household chores, were immortal.

The enigma of Francis was gone too. Because everything was clear now about Francis. Grandy had said so. Grandy had explained his theories at the breakfast table. Jane had agreed. Oliver had agreed. Mathilda had . . . agreed.

She had a little headache this morning. She hadn't slept. She'd been listening in the night. She'd been waiting, in aimless tension, not knowing what she waited for. Briskly tucking in the sheets, Tyl realized that she still had the sensation of expectancy, of waiting for something, an anxiety that wouldn't rest, as if life could not take up, here and now, and go on, and fill in and cover over, with the inexorable wash of time. Although the whole house argued against her and she argued against herself.

Francis was gone. The enigma was explained as well as it ever would be explained. There would be no more to it. The tides of time would wash in every morning and blot and obliterate and smudge and wear down and blur. This day or two, so full of Francis, would recede, would decline in importance, would fade and blur and blend in with all other days of her life. It would be an incident, a queer happening. Once upon a time. Grandy would no doubt make one of his stories out of it. There might even be supernatural overtones before he got through. Mathilda shivered.

Jane wrung out the mop and stood it up in her pail. "I'll help with that," she said, smiling.

How pretty she is, Tyl thought. *I wish I could be just sweet and willing, like Jane.*

They took hold of opposite ends of a blanket. Something was communicated through the length of woolen fabric. Tyl was aware suddenly that Jane was not as she appeared, neither sweet nor willing, not placid at all. Jane was strung up tight. Together, they spread the blanket, tucked it in, folded the sheet back over it, drew up and smoothed the spread.

Tyl said, "Where did he go, Jane?"

Jane said, "He went to the police."

Mathilda sat down on the edge of the freshly made bed. She

looked into Jane's eyes and saw the real girl, saw the hidden fear and sensed the hidden strength.

"Why?" she demanded.

Jane said, "He had things to tell them. If he had got to them, we'd know it. He didn't get there."

Mathilda blinked and groped back. "But you said he'd run away. You said— Grandy said—"

Jane said carefully, "He may have run away. He probably did." She was remote and closed off suddenly. Mathilda didn't want her to be closed off. She wanted to talk. She wanted to know. She wanted the real Jane.

"But you don't believe it," she whispered, "do you?"

"Do you?"

Something that seemed entirely outside of herself shook Mathilda's head for her, shook it in the negative sign. No, she thought, and she hadn't believed it at breakfast, either.

Jane leaned against the bed, bent a little closer. "Can I talk to you and be sure you won't . . . repeat it?"

Mathilda said, "Please."

Jane's doll face didn't belong to a doll any more. "He was in danger. He really was. He was getting too close. How am I going to make you understand?"

"I wish you could," wailed Mathilda. "Because I don't understand anything at all. What danger? What do you think happened to him?"

"I don't know," said Jane, "but something's got to be done. I—" She sat down on the other edge of the bed with her back to Mathilda and covered her face with her hands. "What have I been waiting for?" she said in tones of surprise.

"You're in love with him, aren't you?"

Jane shook her head. Her face was still hidden.

Mathilda said, "But I saw you. Out the window. There's something—"

"What difference does that make?" said Jane fiercely. "Never mind what Francis is to me. Or anybody. Or what he was to Rosaleen. You don't know, and you'll never know, and he's nothing at all to you. Just nothing. But if he's dead now, it'll be because you were so dumb."

"I?"

"I didn't mean that." Jane gulped, turned her face and tried to smile. "I'm worried just about sick."

"Why was I dumb? What do you mean?" Mathilda reached out to shake her.

"I mean he needed your help."

"Then why didn't he ask me or tell me? . . . Help for what?"

"He did. He tried. But you can't see things the way they are. Francis didn't blame you."

"What don't I see?"

"Listen," Jane said, "I was in New York the other day, tracking down something that absolutely proves—"

"Proves what?"

Jane said, "No, I can't tell you."

"Why not?"

"You— Nobody could tell you."

"What's the matter with me, that I can't be told? I'm listening, Jane. Please tell me."

Jane was watching her, searching her face, trying to read it.

Tyl said desperately, "You've got to tell me. I've got to understand, can't you see that? Jane, if you know what this is all about, please—" But Jane seemed to be withdrawing again. "What did you find in New York?" Mathilda begged. "What was it?"

"A record."

"A record?"

"The record they took of a radio program."

"Oh?"

"Yes, I timed it."

"Timed it?"

"It was a question of time. The time was ten thirty-five."

"What time?"

"'Burn tenderly.'"

Mathilda said angrily and bluntly, "I don't understand a word you're saying. You're trying to confuse me. Start at the beginning, why don't you? What are you? Who is Francis?"

"I'm a secretary," said Jane. She shrugged.

"But what are you trying to do? You're in a plot, aren't you? Some kind of plot against—"

Jane lifted her chin.

Mathilda said, faltering, "It's against Grandy, isn't it?"

Jane said, "Do you know that if you repeat any of this conversation, my life won't be worth a nickel? It's worth about ten cents, as it is."

"Oh, nonsense!"

"Is it nonsense?" said Jane. "Where's Fran, then? Why didn't he get to the police station where he was going? What stopped him? Where is he now? Why doesn't he tell us, send some word? Telephone?"

"Because he—because the plot wouldn't work," answered Mathilda weakly.

Jane said bitterly, "You never had a thought in your life. Your mind's been formed for you. You're all wrong about everyone. You don't see straight. It's not your fault. I guess it's your misfortune. You couldn't see Oliver and Althea dancing like puppets on the ends of their strings, could you? You thought they acted for themselves. They didn't any more than you do. Nobody does in this house. Oh, Francis understood. You mustn't think he didn't understand. But he told you there was danger, didn't he?"

"He—"

"And there was danger, and there is danger. He was worried sick about you. You're so blind. And he knew what the danger was." Mathilda was trembling. She was angry and scared. But Jane went on as if to herself, "There's one thing for me to do. There's that man, and I know his name and where he works. And Francis wasn't any helpless girl, you see? So there would have to be a man. That's what he meant" Jane's blue eyes took in Mathilda with a strange, absent look. "You'll spill these beans, of course. My fault. I ought to have known better. Fran warned me. But you looked for a minute as if you'd . . . hear me. But you can't hear me. It isn't your fault."

Suddenly, Jane's voice quickened. "I am glad we talked. I was frozen up, too scared to move, just stuck, just letting things happen. Lord, you can't afford to wait! I guess it's worth any extra danger to get unstuck." Jane's face flamed with resolution. "I'd better get going." She came around the bed. She said, looking down, "Maybe it will work out all right for you sometime. I hope it will." She added gently, "Francis hoped it would, you know."

Jane went out of the room and down the hall to her own.

26

Mathilda fled into the gray room. That which she had been trying not to think about had been spoken out—too plain for her to dodge it any more. She knew now the ridiculous reason, the preposterous—why, the utterly mad reason—for all Francis' lies. First, Francis was mixed up somehow with Rosaleen Wright.

All of a sudden she knew how. Rosaleen had never been one to talk about herself or to confide romantic details. Yet Mathilda had always known that somewhere in the back of Rosaleen's life there was a man she planned to marry someday. Tyl sat down to brood, to think back. She could remember only an impression. This man was an old playmate. A childhood friend, a relative, even—some kind of cousin. It was no flaming romance, but one of those comfortable things. She could remember no name.

Francis? Well, then, Francis thought Rosaleen hadn't killed herself. That was the whole thing. And Jane was in it, too, somehow or other. Certainly, Jane was in love with him. Of course she was. It was perfectly obvious that they were partners. Was Jane a kind of second-string sweetheart?

"Never mind," Jane had said. "He's nothing to you." *Nothing to me*, thought Mathilda, *and what am I to him? Someone to be used in his schemes*? She felt herself in a little glow of anger. Schemes against Grandy. Of all people in the world, dear, kind, lovable Grandy, who wouldn't hurt a fly, wouldn't even hurt your feelings if he could help it.

Surely she knew him best All Grandy's ways, the splendid difference of the way he lived. An amateur of living, he called himself. Lover of life. Oh, he had taught them so much. He'd sent them to carefully chosen schools, but their real education had been in the summers with Grandy. And the world would be stale without him to teach them where its flavor lay.

Why, they wanted to make him out a monster. They wanted to say he was wicked, scheming, unfeeling. Grandy? Grandy, who didn't care about money or any of the stupid material things, who loved, above all, beauty and good food and good talk and ideas. Who believed in the love of these things.

The thought came like a stray. Grandy's fabulous bathroom had cost quite a penny. The love of some kinds of beauty was rather expensive. No, she wrenched at her thoughts. She was off the track. Love. Human love. Grandy believed in love. But he didn't know it when he saw it, said some cynical thing inside her head. He thought Oliver meant security to her. She rubbed her aching forehead.

Someone knocked softly at her door.

"Come in."

"Tyl, darling." And there he was.

Mathilda looked up, startled. There he stood, Grandy himself, his white hair ruffled, as it almost always was, his rather large feet turned out just a little, like the frog footman. His fat little tummy on his thin frame, his big-knuckled hands, his beak of a nose and his sharp black eyes watching her.

She saw him briefly, just in a flash, quite unadorned by her affection. She saw the man standing in her door. She knew he was alert and watchful, and she knew she was not sure, at that moment, of his love. Because she thought of a spider.

"Are you just sitting there?" he asked wonderingly. "Anything troubling?"

Mathilda swallowed. "Headache," she said.

"Ah, too bad." His sympathy was rich and easy for that voice of his. Her heart began to pound. She heard the voice for the first time as a musical instrument played by a mind.

"I won't bother you, sweet. Lie down, eh? There's just the one thing. Yesterday, Francis—"

"Yes?" Her voice shook more than she'd intended.

"Francis showed me a document," he said a little wearily and sadly, "that purported to be your will."

"I know," she said. Her shoulder ached where she pressed it into the back of the chair.

"You know, dear?"

"I mean, he showed it to me, Grandy," she said a bit impatiently. She turned all the way around in the chair and pulled her knees up the other way.

"Another forgery," he sighed.

"Yes."

The black eyes were watching. They were noting her downcast eyes, the nervous interlacing of her fingers. They weren't missing anything. She felt like a bug on a pin. She wanted to squirm and hide, to get away. She bent her head and began to cry.

"Darling." He was very near.

Suddenly, she knew the safest place was nearer still. She wept against his shoulder. She could hide her face there.

"What is the trouble?"

She said, "Grandy, I don't know. The whole thing's so confusing."

He held her off a little, trying to see her eyes. But she kept them hidden.

"I thought you were confused last evening, sweetheart Tyl, what are you trying to tell me?"

"The trouble is," she wailed. "I do— I did—somehow or other remember that minister, Grandy! It's as if I'd seen him before, in a fog or something!"

"Why didn't you tell me?" he said in a moment. "Poor child. And it's been bothering you all the while? You are shaken. That's it, isn't it? Now, you mustn't worry. You really must not."

She felt, in spite of his words, that he was vague. Could he be doubting her, after all? She got hold of her handkerchief and drew away, drying her eyes. "I'm sorry," she said. "It really doesn't mean anything. I really do know that none of what he said was true."

"Of course, you do," Grandy agreed. But his eyes filmed over somehow, and Mathilda had a wild, fantastic, fleeting impression that he was wondering what to do with this self-doubt of hers; not wondering how to dispel it, but how to use it some way.

"Duck, you do not remember writing out any such document as that will, do you?"

"Oh, no," she said. "Oh, no, I never did." He was standing there, looking a bit hurt. She thought she understood. She said, "Oh, Grandy, I'll make another one. I—"

She caught the tiny folding down of flesh at the corner of his eye, the merest trifle of satisfaction.

He said petulantly, "Tyl, you know I want to hear nothing about your money."

"I know," she breathed. But she did not know. She was not sure. The fear was in her veins again, running in a swift thrill from a sinking heart. She did not finish the sentence that had been interrupted. She did not go on to say, "I already have made another will, silly, so we needn't worry about the finest forgery in the world." She didn't say it.

Grandy moved across the room. For one awful second, she thought she had spoken and told him, and then forgotten her own words. She thought her memory had skipped a beat or at least that he'd read her mind. Because he crossed to the little bookshelf and took a book down.

"What a disgraceful collection," he murmured. "My dear, such unfit stuff in this room. I must find you something better."

She was beside him swiftly. "Oh, no. I love Lucile," she said, taking it gently out of his hands. "It's so stuffy and there's a Mathilda in it. And it puts me to sleep."

He chuckled.

"Oh, Grandy," she said. It was on the tip of her tongue to tell him how foolish she'd been, to confess and get it off her soul and be free, where she stood, with no disloyal fear on her conscience. She suffered a complete reaction. The pendulum had swung. Afraid of Grandy! Absurdity of all time! Impossible!

"Now you will tell me the real trouble," he purred, surprising her.

"It's Francis," she murmured.

She hadn't meant to turn her head away or to say that name. She held Lucile in her hands still.

"If anything has happened," she murmured again, "we'd feel so cheap."

"Darling, you are absolutely right!" cried Grandy. "Of course you are! We must take steps, eh?"

"Yes," she said in utter relief.

"Of course we must," said Grandy. "That's only decent, isn't it? For all his sins, Francis was a guest in this house. Yes, I think we must be sure he is not lying in a ditch somewhere. That's what you mean?"

"Oh, Grandy, darling," said Tyl, "you do understand everything!"

Jane's door closed with a little click. They saw Jane in the hall with her blue jacket on over the gingham dress and the little blue cap on her head. She looked quaint and young.

"May I go out for a little while, Mr. Grandison?" she said humbly. "Please, if you don't need me?"

"My dear, of course," he beamed. "Unless it is something I can do for you. I'll be downtown a little later."

"No, I don't think you can, sir," said Jane primly.

"Take the time you need, my dear," said Grandy kindly. "Oh—er—this business about Francis. Tyl thinks we must ask the police to search for him." Jane's face didn't change much. "In case, you know," said Grandy, "he is hurt or dead."

Jane said woodenly, "Of course."

Then she smiled her pretty smile. Her pretty lips formed their pretty thanks. Her feet tripped off. They heard her going down the stairs, not too fast.

But Mathilda knew she flew as one who from the fiend doth fly. She, herself, stood in a backwash of fear. Jane's fear.

Grandy went off to telephone. Mathilda felt disloyal. She felt guilty and soiled. She ought to have told Grandy about Jane. She fidgeted. She went downstairs. Grandy was in the study. The mailman was at the door. She went and opened the door and said, "Good morning." He put a sheaf of letters in her hands.

She said, "Will you do something for me, Mr. Myer? If anything should happen to me, will you look in a book of poetry called Lucile? It's on a shelf in my bedroom."

His mouth dropped open.

"And don't mention what I've said to anyone," she warned, and smiled and closed the door. He stood on the step outside for some time, but at last he went away.

She pulled at her fingers with nervous anxiety. Now she felt disloyal. And guilty. And soiled. But why? What was it now? She mustn't trust Francis. He'd said so himself. She shook her head angrily. She was only doing what he had suggested because she didn't trust him.

Besides, he isn't here, she thought, and she sat down and covered her eyes.

27

THE POLICE were going to check hospitals and all that, and send out a missing-person alarm, Grandy had told her comfortably. It meant that there would be an eye out for Francis for miles around. They would find him, he'd said confidently. Grandy had gone off in his ramshackle car, wearing his old brown hat jauntily.

But Mathilda, waiting alone in the long room downstairs, was not satisfied and far from confident. She wished Jane would come back, or that she knew where Jane was, so that she could go there. There were so many questions Jane could answer. Oliver was in the house, and Mathilda wished he'd go away. He was upstairs and any minute he would probably appear and perhaps he'd want to hash things over. She wished he wouldn't. She wished she weren't alone, but she wished it weren't Oliver who would probably come to keep her company. She wished—wished— She didn't know exactly what it was she wished or what she was waiting for. Vaguely, she was waiting for some word, some news. Did she expect them to find Francis in a hospital? Did she expect them to find him at all? What if they did?

She tried to think, tried to clarify. There were two opinions about the disappearance of Francis. One, that he had run away deliberately, having failed to do whatever he had been attempting to do here. Two, that he had been prevented by violence from getting to the police by someone who didn't want him to get to the police. And, of course, there was a third possibility, which took in all the normal suppositions, that he had been taken ill, he had been in an accident.

She realized that it was the normal kind of disappearance that the police would be able to check, and would be attempting to check now—sudden illness, accident, sudden death. They would also be covering the possibility that he had gone away voluntarily, in which case he wouldn't be hurt at all, but they would find him someday. Through their teletype system, his description, persistent vigilance.

But the possibility they would not cover, and, moreover, had no machinery for covering, was that he had met with malicious violence. For if he had been hidden away, they were not searching in the right kind of place or looking deep enough or close enough, she thought.

She was huddled in the corner of a sofa, as if the room were cold. If only Jane would come back. If only Oliver would come downstairs and not talk, but do something. If only the police would send somebody and start here. If only she could tell someone these thoughts, so that something would be done. She didn't think Grandy had made it clear. Grandy didn't suspect violence.

She began to shiver uncontrollably. She thought, *I'm freezing.* Jane's words came back to her, "Frozen up, just stuck, just letting things happen."

Mathilda uncurled herself and sat up. This was paralysis. She rejected it. She would not wait.

A little later, she was walking down Grandy's drive. The bus for downtown passed within two blocks of Grandy's house. This was one of the city conveniences of which he boasted. The nearest bus stop was obvious. Tyl had no choice to make. She knew this was the way Francis must have come yesterday morning.

She wore her short fur jacket and a little black hat. There was a strong spring breeze blowing her black skirt around her pretty legs. She stood there at the bus stop with her eager, forward-leaning look, and she had no trouble with the bus drivers. They were all glad to lean out as she hailed them, and listen to what she had to say. "Can you remember Thursday morning—yesterday morning? Can you remember if a tall man with dark hair and dark eyes, a youngish man, got on your bus that morning?"

"What time, about, miss?"

"I'm not sure. About ten, I think."

"Lots of people get on and off, miss."

"Oh, I know, but try to remember. He would be wearing a gray coat, I think."

"Not much to go on, miss. Lots of men—"

"Yes, yes, but try! It was at this stop. I'm sure of that. And yesterday morning. Just yesterday. His eyes were dark. His eyebrows—But I guess he wouldn't have been smiling."

"Sorry, miss. Don't think I can help you."

"How many drivers are there on this route?"

"Six, miss."

"Thank you."

She tried again with the next driver and the next. The fourth man sucked his lip and said, "What do you want to know for?"

"Oh, because he was going somewhere, and he never got there, and I've been wondering."

The driver said, "Maybe I got your man. A fellow that changed his mind."

"He . . . did?"

"Yeah, yesterday morning. Tall, you say?"

"Tall, dark."

"I wouldn't wanta say he was dark. I wouldn't have noticed. But there was a tall fellow in a gray coat waiting here, only he didn't get on."

"He didn't?"

"No. Just as I was pulling up, a fellow comes up behind him—friend of his, I guess. So he turns around and goes off with the other guy. Gets in his car, see? The other guy notices him and picks him up. Happens all the time. People getting a lift. That help you any?"

"He went off with a friend?" said Mathilda incredulously.

The bus driver thought she was a stunner. "Listen, miss, I only said he was a friend. How do I know? All I know is, this guy didn't get on my bus. He was waiting for the bus, see, but he don't get on, on account of this other guy."

"Did you notice the other guy?"

"Gosh." The driver pushed at his cap. The passengers were shuffling in their seats. He couldn't chat any longer. "I dunno. Nothing special I can remember. But they got in this D.P.W. car."

"What's that?"

The door began to wheeze shut "D.P.W.! Department of Public Works!" he shouted at her. The bus moved off.

D.P.W. D.P.W. Mathilda stood on the empty corner and looked around her. Houses here were set in fat lawns, far apart, well back from the street. Nobody was about or would have been.

Wait, there was someone across the street. A gardener doing some spring pruning. She ran across. She fetched up the outer side of the hedge and the man stopped his work.

"Please, were you working here yesterday?"

"Nah."

"Oh," she said, disappointed. She turned away.

"Whatsa matter, lady?"

"I only wondered if you'd seen a certain car," she said. "But if you weren't here—"

"I was over at Number Sixty-eight," he said, and spat.

"Where?"

"Over there." His thumb showed her the neighboring lawn. "I work there Thursdays. Here Fridays."

"Oh, then maybe you did see it! There was a car with D.P.W. on it. Yesterday morning."

"Yeah," he said, and spat again.

"You saw it!"

"Sure I saw it."

"Did two men get in?"

"Yeah." There was something curious and yet reserved in his glance, as if he could tell her something if she had the wit to ask, but would not offer it.

"One of the men was waiting for the bus?"

"I couldn't say about that."

"It doesn't matter. I want to know where—which way did the car go?"

He pointed.

"That way?"

"Yeah."

"Did it go straight on? Did it turn?" She thought, *I'll never be able to do this. This is hopeless.*

"Turned left on Dabney Street," he told her surprisingly.

"Oh! Oh, thank you!" She started to run, stopped, looked back. "Was there anything—anything more you noticed?"

A curtain dropped in his interested eyes. "Nah, I didn't notice anything," he said.

But she thought, *He did. There was something about it, something queer.*

She thanked him again and walked briskly in the direction of the Dabney Street corner. Now what to do? Now, ought she to call the police? Tell them about that car? Surely they could trace all cars so marked. Those cars must belong to the city. She ran back again.

The gardener hadn't begun to clip yet. He was just standing there, looking after her.

"One thing more," she gasped. "It was a car from this town? I mean it was the D.P.W. here?"

"Sure," he said. "That's right." He pulled his disreputable hat down and began to work his clippers very fast, moving around a shrub with the deepest concentration on his task.

Mathilda started down the street again. At Dabney Street, she turned left, as had the car with Francis in it. That is, the car she thought Francis had been in. It seemed probable that he'd been in it. At least, it was possible. She walked a few paces, out of the gardener's sight at least. And then, at a loss, she stood still.

The pavement told her nothing. How could it? The houses here were a little less aloof, a little more chummy with the street, but still— A car passed yesterday morning. What remains to tell you that it has passed or where it went, which corners, after this, it turned, which way?

She felt very small and helpless. There was no use walking along Dabney Street. No use, she thought.

There was a little boy in leggings and jacket, sitting on his three-wheeled bike, watching her. He was part way up the walk of the first house around the corner. He was about three years old.

Mathilda started toward him. She would ask. She thought, *No, how silly! It's just a baby!* She stood irresolutely at the opening between hedges, the end of the walk where he was.

The door of the house beyond him opened suddenly and his mother appeared, rather suspiciously, as if she thought this strange young woman might have designs on her child. She hurried down the walk, wearing only her house dress, moving fast in the chilly spring air.

"Gigi . . ."

Gigi kept on looking at Tyl.

"Let me see your hands." He surrendered his dirty little paws. The woman began to put her fingers into the tiny pockets of his snowsuit. She looked over her shoulder at Tyl. "Was there anything you wanted?" she inquired with a polite grimace.

"I . . ." Tyl gulped. "I did want to find out something," she said, "but I don't know quite how to go about it. I was going to ask your little boy, but I'm afraid he's too little to remember."

"Remember what?"

"Just . . . whether a certain car went by yesterday morning."

"He wouldn't know," said the mother sternly.

"No, I guess he wouldn't," said Tyl. She turned away.

"You come right in and let me wash those hands," she heard the woman saying. "Where in the world . . . ! You didn't get into any *more* chocolate, did you?"

"Uhuh," said Gigi.

"You didn't pick anything up and put it in your mouth *today?*"

"Uhuh."

"You remember what Mommy told you? *Did* you?"

"Umum."

"He doesn't know," said the woman apologetically to Tyl, who still stood uncertainly on the sidewalk. "Lord, he'll pick up any old thing and it's *so* dangerous. Gigi, I *told* you to throw that paper *away*."

The woman pulled something out of the little pocket and threw it on the ground.

Gigi bawled protest.

"You *cannot* have it! You *mustn't* keep dirty old things other people have thrown away. How *many* times . . . ?"

But Mathilda was at her elbow now, breathless, demanding. "When did he find the chocolate? Was it yesterday?"

"Yes, it was," the woman said in surprise.

"Oh, thank you!" cried Mathilda. "Thank you so much! That's just what I wanted to know!"

She swooped down and picked up the bit of bright metallic paper, gaudy enough to attract a child, bright enough to see in the grass. She flattened it out with eager fingers. There was the Dutch name hidden in the pattern. It was a wrapper from one of Grandy's chocolates!

Francis, in her room that night, had taken a handful. He'd put them in his pocket. No one on earth but Francis or Grandy could have dropped one of those candies. And there was a car that had turned on Dabney Street, that had picked up a man who had waited for a bus.

Francis! It was a trail! It was going to be a paper chase! Oh, clever Francis!

"Oh, thank you! Thank you so much!" Tyl flew back down the path. The woman stood in belated curiosity.

But Tyl went off down Dabney Street with the paper in her pocket and her fingers tight on it. Oh, clever Francis! But this showed he hadn't got into that car because he wanted to. Or why drop clues?

28

Perhaps he had taken it out to eat it. Perhaps he had dropped it by accident. Perhaps somebody else, after all, had Dutch chocolates. But no, no, no. *At least*, she thought, *I've got to go on down Dabney Street and keep looking.*

She kept her eyes along the curb, remembering that Francis would have been the passenger, would have been sitting on this side. Still, it was yesterday. Other children on the street might have found other candies, and how would she know? She thought of Hansel and Gretel, of the birds that ate the crumbs and spoiled the trail home.

She came to the next corner and stopped to think it out. A car turning a corner keeps to the right. Francis sat on the right. She went around the corner to the right, searching the inside curb. Nothing. Then she thought that if the car turned left, he would be on the outside. The middle of the intersection was no good. She crossed over and searched along the curb near which Francis would have been carried had the car turned left. Nothing.

Now what to do? She saw the search branching out hopelessly. Now she had a choice of three, and each corner she would reach on each of three routes would have, in turn, a choice of three. The thing multiplied violently. It was impossible.

She went along Dabney Street, walking on down on the right side, watching the curb. He had dropped a clue, hadn't he, after they'd turned a corner? He wouldn't drop a clue at every cross street. So, at every intersection she searched, after the turns. Six blocks along, she saw a bit of burnished purple. Intact. Candy and all. Another one! The car had turned right on Enderby Street. Oh, clever Francis! Oh, clever Mathilda! She walked along jauntily, happy and pleased and excited. She knew where to look now, for sure.

She found a green wrapper twisted up, empty, on the brink of a sewer. Her lip began to bleed where she'd bitten it, thinking how near that clue had been to being lost. Head down, she plodded on. She spotted a blue one from all the way across the road. She thought, *My eyes are good. They'll last as long as the candies do*. She wondered how many there could have been in that handful. And how many more corners—

She plodded on. Ten blocks on the same street. She stopped, then, and went back in a panic. She'd missed it. Or it was gone. She came along the same ten blocks again, almost despairing. Nothing.

On the eleventh corner there was a purple one shining under a hedge. To the left, then. *Yes, Francis*. Eyes aching, she went on. The trail had led her into a meaner part of town, a poorer part, at least. A part where she'd never been. Not on foot. Not alone. Surely the afternoon must be wearing along. This street seemed to have uneasy shadows. The trail had been so long. She looked at her watch. No, it was not even two o'clock.

She stopped in her tracks. Her eye just caught it. She would have been by in another second. Inside the driveway, inside the straggly border of barberry bushes, there was a little heap of five or six candies all together. Bright and gay, like Christmas, they sparkled on the dull grass. Inside the drive. Inside the property line.

The house was a dirty white, an old frame house, respectable enough, closed looking. No sign of children here, no flowers, no outdoor life at all. A bleak porch, a tall door with old-fashioned hardware.

She made herself walk by, hiding as well as she could her sudden stop by pretending to search in her purse, as if she'd thought of something. She walked two doors beyond. Shrubs, just leafing out, hid her now. She stopped again. That was the house! In there. The thing to do was to call the police, of course. But would they come? Would they believe her? Would they be quick enough? Would they go into the house? Could she convince them there was enough to warrant going in?

She thought, *If I could only get closer.*

She dared not go to the door and ring and make an excuse. If Francis was in there, he would not, in any case, be sitting in the front parlor to be seen by a caller. He would not answer the door, either. That wouldn't be any good.

She turned slowly back and went, instead, up the walk to the neighbor house. There was a deep shrub border between the plots. She had an idea.

The lady of the house was at home.

"I beg your pardon," Tyl said with all the charm she could muster. "I want to ask you a strange kind of favor. You see, the other day my little boy and I were coming by, and he lost his ball. His favorite ball."

"Isn't that a shame," said the woman. She had a long flat jaw, and she pulled it far down, as if she were making a face. She meant well, Mathilda realized.

"Yes, it was too bad," she continued, "and I was just going by again, and I thought perhaps you'd let me look in among your shrubs there. I'll be very careful. I won't injure them; really I won't."

"Well, I guess you won't," the woman said rather grudgingly.

"Then you don't mind if I poke around in there a little? If I could find it, he'd be so happy. He's three," she babbled. "His name is Gigi. That's what I call him. I would be so grateful to you."

"Go ahead," said the woman harshly, as if she washed her hands of the whole thing.

"Oh, thank you."

"Don't mention it."

The door drew shut slowly. Tyl thought, *She'll go to a window. She's watching, remember.*

Slowly, she went across the narrow strip of lawn and peered on the ground along the edge of the border of mock orange and straggly overgrown lilac and shabby privet. She bent her head to appear to look at the ground, but her eyes were directed higher.

She looked up under her brows to inspect the shabby white frame house, so near, actually, in distance, although the fact of the shrubbery border set it apart from where she stood. There was only a driveway and then a narrow strip of ground with rhododendrons, and then the white house wall, the stone foundation.

Shades were drawn in the stingy bay of the front room on this side. The next window was high—on the stairs, probably. Two windows farther back would be the kitchen, and that would be dangerous.

She stepped within the shrub border, moving slowly, stirring leaves and sticks with her foot, but watching next door. She was disappointed. There really was no way to see in from this side. The bay was high and the shades were drawn close. She wouldn't dare to try to see into the kitchen, and besides, it was too high. The stair window would be no good at all without a ladder. In the stonework, however, below, there was a little window, down back of the rhododendrons.

She thought, *So my little boy's ball might have gone into the rhododendrons. Mightn't it? Do I dare?* She thought, *I must. They won't see me. Nobody sits on the stairs. The kitchen's too far back.*

She went stooping through the shrubs, crossed the invisible boundary line between the lots, moved quietly across the hard-surfaced driveway, kept her head down, kept her movements tentative, groping, wandering, but edging herself to that cellar window.

Francis was lying on his right side now. When Mrs. Press had brought him food, he had wiggled around. She had crouched over him, feeding him carelessly, not caring much whether he got the food in his mouth or on his vest. His mouth was stiff and sore. It was agony to try to eat, but he did try. He didn't speak to the woman. She didn't speak either. He felt about her as he might have felt about a sleeping dog. He didn't want to awaken her to being aware of him. He wanted her to feed him carelessly, as if it were only another chore. He didn't want that look back in her eye. So she had put the gag back in efficiently and gone away, and now he was lying on his right side, which was a change.

Press himself had not been down. If only Press could be reached. What if he knew that Grandy, too, was a murderer already? For Press was a murderer already and Grandy knew it. That much was clear to Francis now. Press was one of the unsuspected, perhaps the one the old man had in his mind that day on the radio. That was why he had to do what Grandy said.

But what if Press knew they were even? Would he obey then? If only Press could be told. But how, even if the man did come, could Francis explain all this, lying, as he was, speechless and gagged? The light was flickering.

What light? Daylight. That was the only light at all. Murky daylight from the dirty little window, and it flickered. He rolled his eyes. He saw a hand on the glass. Someone was crouching down outside the window, trying to see in. He lifted both heels from the cement floor and dropped them with a thud. He did it again.

Again. The fingers curled. They tapped twice. He made the thud with his heels twice. He nearly choked, forgetting to breathe.

The fingers went away and came back. They expressed emotion, somehow. Whoever it was knew now. He could make out the shadows of arm movements. Fur. A woman.

The little window was nailed tightly shut.

Outside, Mathilda crouched behind the rhododendrons. She couldn't see clearly at all, only the barest glimpse of a bare floor where a little light fell. The window was too dirty. The place inside too dark.

But she had heard. She had signaled. She had been answered. The little window was locked tightly, nailed shut. She took off her shoe and struck the glass with the heel. It tinkled on the floor inside, so faint a sound she was sure it couldn't have been heard. She put her mouth up close to the opening, "Francis?"

Francis strained at the gag. His throat hurt with the need to answer. He tapped with his heels. It was all he could do.

"Francis? Can you hear?"

Tap again. Raise your ankles and let the heels fall.

"Can't you talk?"

Tap again. Tap twice.

"Tap twice for 'no,'" she whispered. "Once for 'yes.'"

He didn't tap at all.

"Can't you talk?"

He tapped twice for "no."

"But you're Francis?"

He tapped once for "yes."

"Thank God!" she said. "Are you hurt?"

"No."

"What shall I do?"

No taps. How could he answer?

"Can I get in?"

"No."

"I'd better go for help?"

"Yes."

"Are you in danger?"

"Yes." *Oh, Mathilda, so are you. Go away, quickly.* All he could do was tap once for "yes."

"I'll get help. I'll get the police."

"Yes!"

Tyl, he wanted to cry, *don't get Grandy. Of all people, keep away from him. Don't even tell him you've found me. Tyl, if you really do thank God, then hurry. Go to the police, the public authorities, to someone safe. Go away now, before that woman sees you. Go silently. Don't run yourself slam bang into danger. Don't run. Oh, Tyl, be careful. Take care of yourself.*

"I'll hurry," she said. He had an illusion that she'd heard him thinking. He raised his heels, tapped "yes."

"Don't worry," she said.

He couldn't answer that one. Worry! God, would he worry. Oh, clever Tyl. She'd followed the trail. She'd found it. But he couldn't talk, he couldn't warn her, he couldn't say— If only she would go now, silently, quickly, straight to the public authorities. If only he could have told her so.

There was hope now—too much hope. It was terrifying. Hope and fear. He was afraid for her. He almost wished she hadn't found him. He rolled his head on the floor painfully. He groaned beneath the gag. He almost wished for the peace of hopelessness.

29

Mathilda went back through the shrubbery border. She stooped once, remembering, and pretended to pick up something, in case the woman next door should still be at a window somewhere.

Then she let herself move faster, went out onto the lawn and the street. She walked a little way. Then she began to run, gasping, heart pounding. Only get far enough away and then find a telephone. She was a little deaf and blind with excitement and haste. She didn't see or hear the rattling old car until it honked a surprised little squawk at her and pulled up at the curb. "Tyl! Tyl!" Her body didn't want to stop running. She had to will the brakes on.

"Tyl, what is the matter? Darling!"

And there was Grandy, tumbling out of his car, fumbling at his pince-nez to keep them on. Dear Grandy! He would know what to do! She'd forgotten everything but that she was in haste and Francis must be saved, and here was Grandy, to whom she had told all her troubles all her remembered life.

She threw herself upon him. Wept with relief. "Grandy, I found Francis! I found him! Something awful has happened!"

"Hush," he said. "Hush, Tyl. Now tell me quietly."

"Oh, Grandy, help me find a policeman! Somebody to get him out! Because he's in there! He's in there!"

"In where?"

"In that cellar! He's tied up! He can't talk! Oh Grandy, quick, let's get somebody!"

He held her, supporting her. "You say you've found Francis? Are you quite sure?"

"Of course, I'm sure! It is! Oh, Grandy, be quick!"

"But where, dear?"

"That house back there. The white one. Can you see? The first white one, with the reddish bush. That's where he is. In the cellar. I saw through the window. What shall we do?"

"Get the police," said Grandy promptly. "Tyl, darling, how did you— Look here. Are you sure?"

"I'm positive!"

"But did anyone see you?"

"I don't know. So hurry!"

"But how could you tell it was—"

"I broke the glass."

"Tyl, darling."

"Oh, hurry!" she sobbed. "Because he's in danger!"

He said, "Yes. This is bad business, isn't it?" Now he was matter-of-fact, no longer surprised. He sounded cool and brisk and capable. "Tyl, do you think you could take the car and go find a telephone? There's a drugstore a block down, or two blocks down—somewhere down there. You go call the police. Call headquarters. Ask for Gahagen himself. Can you manage?"

"Yes, I can," she said.

"While I go back and keep an eye on that house."

"Oh, yes!" she agreed gladly. "Oh, Grandy, that's right! Oh, yes, do! You stay and watch. Watch out for Francis."

"That's what I'll do," he said gently. "Go to the drugstore, duckling. Call from a booth. We can't have this all over town,"

"Give me a nickel," she said resolutely.

He gave her a nickel. Watching her, he knew she would obey the suggestions. She would go to the drugstore. She would ask for Gahagen. It would all take time.

Mrs. Press opened the back door suspiciously. Then she let the door go wide, recognizing him.

"What have you got to put him in?" said Grandy briskly, without introduction.

"There's a trunk," she said.

"Get it."

"It's upstairs."

"Drag it down."

Recognizing emergency, she went without saying anything more. Grandy called a number on the telephone.

"Press?"—crisply. "Can you send a truck here in the next five minutes? Trouble. Police. Tell them to pick up a trunk." Sharply: "If you can't do it in five minutes, there's no use." Coldly: "You realize what will happen if you don't, this being your house?" Calmly: "Yes, I hoped you would. Tell them it's full of germs. Yes, germs. Typhoid. Anything."

Grandy hung up the phone. There was a loud bumping and crashing. He went into the stair hall and helped Mrs. Press with the big old empty turtleback trunk.

The two of them went down for Francis. Even with his limbs bound, even gagged and stiff and sore as he was, they had no easy time. Francis was sick at heart. This hurry, this wild anxiety of haste, could only mean that Tyl had made contact somewhere, somehow, and Grandy had found it out. So it was to be no good? No soap? Not even now, after she'd found him and thanked God? He would not see her face again, to thank her or to explain or just to see her face again?

He was damned if he wouldn't! The woman had great strength,

and Grandy was not so weak an old man as he, perhaps, looked. They were desperate and in a hurry. They got him up the cellar steps, although all the way he bucked like a bronco. The scene in the hall was dreadful in its grim wordlessness. It was a voiceless battle of desperations. The yawning trunk was like a tomb, and the living man, in all his helplessness, refused to go.

But he fell. He fell out of their weakening grasp, and he had no arms. He struck his head. They folded him over, jammed him in, stuffed him down.

The woman, panting, said, "Better do it!"

Grandy screeched, "No time! No time!"

They shut the lid down. Grandy took the key and turned it in the lock. Together, they dragged again, tipped the bulky object over the front doorsill. Mrs. Press closed the door.

"With a knife," she gasped, "it wouldn't have taken long!"

Grandy said "Blood?" He sneered at her stupidity. Then he warned her, "You don't know anything, when you're asked." He looked no more than a trifle worried now, a bit flustered. His frenzy was gone.

"I don't know anything," she said contemptuously. She watched him go back toward the kitchen. She heard the soft closing of the kitchen door.

The police car came wailing down the street to where Tyl stood, hopping with anxiety, on the drugstore corner. It barely stopped. It snatched her up. She showed them the way and told them as much as she could in the few brief noisy minutes it took them to swoop on, five blocks—the drugstore had been farther away than Grandy had said—down the street.

When the big, clumsy gray garbage truck came rumbling along, going in the opposite direction, the men on top, in their dusty boots and aprons and heavy gloves, looked wonderingly down. They leaned against the big trunk balanced there, the last of their load.

Chief Blake, who was driving himself, dodged by with a skillful twist and a brief snarl of his siren.

30

THE CAR came to a skidding stop. One uniformed man went in a jogging run down the drive to the back of the house. Chief Blake and the other went up on the front porch. Tyl slid off Gahagen's lap, where she scarcely knew she'd been sitting, hit the ground with both feet. Grandy was nowhere to be seen.

"Got the right house?"

"Oh, yes! Yes!" She looked for him on all sides.

Then Grandy rose up out of the shrub border there by the driveway. He had old leaves in his hair. A smudge of earth streaked across his cheek. He came toward them. He was beaming.

"Lurking Luther never took his eye off!" His thin lips smiled out the silly words. "It is there as it was there!" He made a flat triumphant sweep with his palm. "Not a soul stirred. Not a soul saw me. I lay low, by gum, I did! What an afternoon, at my age! I had no idea how fascinating it is to put one's ear literally to the ground. Oh, cowboys! Oh, Indians!"

Gahagen grinned. "Your little girl's upset."

"But the marines are landing," said Grandy, "eh? Now, how do you do this, Tom? This is most fascinating. Beard 'em, don't you? Do we break down the door? I'd like to see that. I never believe it in the movies."

Mathilda's heart ached. She felt tired out, all of a sudden. Grandy could set a mood; he always did. But this mood struck her wrong. It jangled. It hurt.

"We try ringing the front doorbell first," said Gahagen. "Come on."

Chief Blake said, "How d'ya do, Mr. Grandison? What goes on here?"

"That's what we wonder," said Grandy, "and we do wonder, don't we?"

The chief was a big solid fellow, the type to be slow and sure—especially sure. "We'll find out," he promised.

A thin woman opened the door and stood looking hostilely at them. "Well?" Thin and drab and sour, she wasn't afraid of them or even particularly interested. "Well?" she snapped.

"We want to look in your cellar," said Blake, in all his huge simplicity.

"What for?"

"This young lady saw a man tied up down there."

The woman's eyes were not so drab as the rest of her. They examined Tyl with contempt and curiosity. "There's nobody in the cellar," she said. "I don't know what you're talking about."

"But there is!" began Tyl.

Grandy's hand warned her to keep calm, reminded her that they were among the officers of the law and all would proceed in due order.

"We'll take a look, if you don't mind," said Blake, and one felt that it would come to pass as he had said.

The woman surrendered to that certainty. "I guess I can't stop you," she said ungraciously.

The other uniformed man stood on guard where he was, there at the front door. The rest of them followed the woman into the house, down the dingy brown hall, past the doors to the sitting room, past a dining-room door. The cellar steps went down opposite here.

The woman opened the door and snapped on a light for them as if she said, "You fools!"

Tyl went down too.

There was a little furnace room, cluttered with old boxes, not neat. It smelled of stale wine and coal gas. Tyl looked up and saw the woman, standing above them with her hot, angry eyes fixed on Chief Blake's burly back.

There were two doors out of here, one to a laundry. Gahagen opened that and peered in, closed it again. They all turned to the second door. It was not locked. It led to a perfectly empty room.

"Any more rooms down here?" the chief said. His voice boomed.

"The cellar don't go under the hull house!" the woman called shrilly. "There's nobody down there! I told you!"

Mathilda stood in the empty little room and looked around at the stone walls. It was gloomy. Someone found the light. She blinked as the bare bulb sprang into glowing life.

"Where would the place be?" Chief Blake looked down at her. "Which side of the house, Miss Frazier, eh?"

"Mrs. Howard," said Grandy softly.

She felt her heart sink down—that sick, falling feeling. The taste of fear rose in her throat. Why did Grandy put that in? The fiction of her marriage? Why did he want them to think— She couldn't understand.

She moistened her lips. "It was right here," she said. Her voice was too thin. It piped up like a child's voice. "Here," she repeated, "because, don't you see, that's the window I broke?"

They all looked up. Sure enough. The window was broken.

"Now—uh—you say you saw him?" Chief Blake shifted around to face her—grill her, she thought.

"I couldn't see very well," she admitted, "but it was Francis, because he answered me."

"You talked to him, eh?"

"He couldn't talk, but—"

"But you say he answered. What do you mean by that, Miss—er—"

"He did. You see, he could make a kind of thudding noise somehow. Like a heavy tap on the floor. So—" She swallowed. It didn't even sound plausible to her. It sounded ridiculous, and yet it was true.

"It's true!" she cried aloud. "He did answer me! He pounded once for 'yes' and twice for 'no.' I asked if it was Francis!"

"Pounded, eh?" Chief Blake seemed to take what she said perfectly literally, and he looked about him.

Tom Gahagen said, "Maybe you weren't as smart as you thought you were, Luther. Could be, you were seen. Better search the whole place. . . . What d'ya say, Blake?"

"If the young lady's so sure—"

"I'm absolutely sure!" Mathilda told them desperately.

So the house was searched. She went along. She had to see it for herself. The cellar. They thumped the stone walls. They shifted the low pile of coal with a long shovel. Then the kitchen, cupboards, pantry. The dining room. She saw Gahagen lift the long tablecloth and look under. It struck her as absurd, as if a man like Francis were a child, hiding from them. They searched the sitting room. Not there. They looked thoroughly into the clothes closet in the hall.

The woman of the house stood by, against walls. She followed along and stood contemptuously back and watched. She was arrogant and sulky and sure.

"There's nobody here," she kept saying.

They went upstairs. Three bedrooms, more closets, a bath—a

cubbyhole off the hall. No living thing. No dead thing, either. No person at all. They asked about the attic. There was a ladder to let down, and they let it down and a man went up. He came back sneezing.

"Nobody up there," he said.

And that was all there was to the house.

Chief Blake looked sidewise at Tyl's white face. "Try the garage."

The garage was cold and vacant. Just a tin shack. Nobody, nothing in it.

The men poked about the little back yard, lifted the slanting cellar doors with sudden energy and let them down again, slowly. There was nobody in the house or on the grounds except the woman, who stood on the porch now to watch in contemptuous silence.

"Well," said Gahagen. He let his shoulders fall helplessly. He looked at Mathilda. They all did.

"But I know he was here!" she said.

"He's not here now, miss," said one of the men.

"But he was. . . . Grandy!" she wailed for help.

"How long before you met Luther and sent him back to stand watch?" asked Gahagen sharply.

"Not long," she faltered. "A m-minute."

They shook their heads. They shrugged.

She wanted to scream.

"If you're through, I'd be obliged if you'd leave," the woman said, from the porch, her voice thin and dry with her contempt.

Tyl turned to her. "What happened?" she cried. "You know! . . . Mr. Gahagen, don't you see she must know? Why don't you make her tell?"

"Why, you—" The woman's eyes blazed. "Call me a liar?"

"Hush, hush," said Grandy. . . . "Tyl, darling, it's possible you were mistaken."

She moistened her lips. "No."

The woman said, "Now you seen what you seen, you better all get out of here." She went indoors contemptuously.

Grandy looked at Gahagen. "Perhaps Mathilda's overwrought—" His voice was gentle and sad.

"I'm not!" cried Tyl, knowing that the squeal of desperation in her tone denied her words. "I'm not." She tried to make it sound firm and sane.

"Oh, my dear"—in pity.

"Francis was here!"

"Hush."

Tyl thought, *I won't scream. I won't cry*. She said, "How could I have been mistaken? I told you about the candy."

"Candy? What candy was that, Miss Frazier—Mrs.—" Chief Blake would Listen.

"Candy!" she cried. "That's how I trailed him! He dropped pieces of candy, like a paper chase. . . . They were some of your Dutch chocolates, Grandy. That's how I found the house. Did you think I went looking in every cellar window? Come out here to the front. I'll show you." Her voice rang with new confidence.

But on the dull grass, just emerging from its winter brown, there was no glittering little heap of candies now. There was nothing there. Nothing on the grass anywhere.

They stood and looked at the ground. Gahagen scraped with his sole, made a mark.

Grandy said softly, "Come home, Tyl."

"No."

"He isn't here, dear. You saw that."

"But he was!" she wailed. "Because I know he was! Grandy, you believe me, don't you?"

"There, there. Hush."

"This is the little girl that was on the ship?" Chief Blake was asking delicately.

She knew Grandy was nodding. She knew glances flew, now, above her head.

"She's been under a strain," Grandy said in his soothing way. His voice stroked and patted at the situation, stretching it here, pushing at lumps. He was going to cover over this indecency of the impossible. Everything would seem reasonable and able to be believed, after he had stroked the facts with his voice a while. "Dreadful strain," he was murmuring. "First that, and then Althea's death. Her own sister couldn't have been closer. And now, you see, her husband has gone off without leaving any word. It's no wonder. Poor child."

They were murmuring too. She could hear the hum of their consent and understanding.

"It's all been terribly confusing," Grandy said. "I can't even tell you all of it. But she really— It's no wonder if her senses begin to play her tricks. I think if you'd been through . . . stresses and the bewildering circumstances—" His voice murmured off, died in wordless sympathy.

Tyl felt frozen and trapped.

Her senses. Here it was again. She did not know what she knew she knew. Here was Grandy saying so! What Francis had said! She did not know what had happened. What she thought she saw, couldn't be trusted. What she thought she remembered, no one else remembered, and even inanimate things shifted and changed behind her back. Because her senses played her tricks? Did they, in fact? She didn't know, herself, at the moment. She wasn't sure any more.

Gahagen said cheerfully, "No harm done."

Blake said kindly, "Just as well to make sure. Say, that's all right."

"Never mind, little girl. We understand," their voices said.

She stood still in utter terror. What it meant, her mind didn't know. But her body was sick with fear.

A taxicab pulled up abruptly. A girl got out. The girl was Jane. She came to them quickly. She was decisive and demanding.

"What is it?" said Jane. "What are all of you doing here?"

31

The group shifted to let Jane in. There was a reluctance to say what they were doing here. No one volunteered.

"Ah, Jane, dear child," said Grandy. . . . "Gentlemen, this is my little secretary, from the house. . . . Look, dear, let us take Mathilda home in your cab."

"But wait a minute—"

"I thought Francis was in there," Mathilda said wearily. "I thought I'd found him."

The blond girl's eyes didn't flinch from hers. "That's strange," she said. "Because this is where Press lives."

"Press?" Grandy said it

"Yeah, the name here is Press, all right," said Chief Blake.

"You mean Ernie Press?"

"Yeah."

"Why, I am acquainted with him," said Grandy. "Of course. Do you mean to tell me—"

Jane said crisply, "I'd like to know what this is about, please."

There was a shocked little silence, the result of her rudeness. Then Gahagen began to tell her.

Mathilda felt strength seeping back into her spine. Jane was no baby doll or child, either. Jane had force. Jane made sense. She listened eagerly. It was a different kind of sense from Grandy's, but sense. Something clear.

Tyl said, "Yes, and I did communicate, Jane. He did answer me."

"Let me tell you something," said Jane in her clear and surprisingly bold voice. "Francis warned me that if anything ever happened to him, I should look up this man named Press."

This was odd. Tyl felt the balance shift. She could tell that they were checked, turned back, made to think again.

"He works for the city," went on Jane. "The D.P.W."

"D.P.W.!" cried Mathilda. "Of course! Yes, yes! Francis got into his car. His car, Jane! It had D.P.W. on it Ask the gardener."

Grandy bent forward, as if he drew a line across Tyl's eagerness to cancel it. "But of course Press works for the city," he purred. "Of course he does, child."

Jane paid him no heed. She went on, "I've been watching Mr. Press. He's been at his office down in the city yard. A little while ago he left suddenly. And very fast. He drove to the corner of Mercer Lane. That's about four blocks up and over." Jane pointed. "I followed him there."

"My dear Jane!" murmured Grandy with astonishment, and still she paid him no heed. Jane was a doll without any strings. Mathilda stood straighter.

"He spoke to the driver of a garbage truck," said Jane.

They all looked blank.

"The truck started up right away. It turned off. I followed Press again, until I found out he was only going back to his office. Then I thought I'd see what that truck did. Did it come here?"

"Eh?" said Grandy. He looked thunderstruck.

"Did it?" said Jane. "Because it turned this way." Her blue eyes were stern and clear. One would have to answer.

"Oh, me!" said Grandy. "I didn't see any garbage truck."

"Mr. Grandison was watching the house," Blake explained with his monumental patience, "the entire time, or practically so, between when Miss—er—the young lady says she saw—"

"Oh, he was!" said Jane with peculiar emphasis.

Tyl's pulse was racing. She thought she saw how everything could be reconciled. "No, no. Maybe he didn't see it!" she cried. "But it could have come along just the same. He might not have seen it People don't. It's like a waiter. You don't see his face."

"Like the postman!" said Grandy quickly, almost as if he clutched at a straw. "Oh, my dear, can I be guilty of that stupidity? Chesterton's Invisible Man! You remember, Tom. You've read those things. The invisible people who come and go in the street and are not seen because you are so used to them. Now, I couldn't say—I really couldn't say whether I saw a garbage truck—"

"Suppose the dame in the house saw you, Luther," Gahagen offered. "She tips off her husband."

"Yes," said Grandy. He drawled out some doubt. "Yees."

"He sends a truck around."

"But, Tom—"

"Listen. He's the guy who knows exactly where those trucks are, all day, every day. They got a map and schedules. You'd be surprised. Say a lady loses her ring or a piece of good silver in the trash. Happens often. Why, he can stop the truck before they dump."

"Dump?" said Jane, her hand on her throat. "Dump?"

"Yeah, they dump down at the incinerator."

"Is that a fact?" said Grandy. "They do know, then, exactly where each truck—"

"Sure, it's a fact."

"Yeah, but what's the idea here?" said Blake. He slowed them down. He fixed on Jane. "You're saying, miss, that this man Press sends around a garbage truck to pick up a man?"

Jane swayed on her feet. "He sent a truck somewhere."

"And the man's gone," said Mathilda in a clear, bold voice. She stood by Jane. "He was helpless. He couldn't speak. He couldn't yell. He could have been carted away." Jane's shoulder leaned on hers. The girls were side by side. It was a lining up of forces.

"Now look here," said Grandy reasonably. Everyone turned to him. "I do understand that Press is in a position to—let us say—summon a garbage truck. I know that. I concede as much. In fact, I remember now that he had spoken of the system with which they run their noisome affairs. It's truly remarkable—truly—the things that go on in the background of our lives and we reck not of; we are unaware—"

Jane said, "What are you going to do?"

She said it to the others. Grandy went on smoothly, as if she had not done the unforgivable again and interrupted him, "I do not understand what it is you—er—imagine, Jane, my dear. How can a man's body be taken away on a garbage truck? You aren't saying that the men on the truck are all in cahoots? Now come. What had Francis done, ever, to the Department of Public Works?"

Jane said, "The incinerator." She lost all color. "The fires are so very hot!" Her face was dead white.

Tyl said, "They wouldn't— No! Where is the incinerator? . . . Jane, come on!"

"Wait."

"No."

"Girls, girls, you can't—"

Tyl cried out, "Somebody's got to—" Jane's hand was on her arm, gripping tightly. They were allied. They ran toward the taxi. Gahagen leaped after them.

Chief Blake said, hastily for him, apologetically, "Maybe we better run down there."

32

The taxi driver was delighted to be on official business and go as fast as he could go. Jane and Tyl and Gahagen rocked in the seat, bracing themselves. Jane's hand and Tyl's were welded together. There was no use trying to talk. Now and then, Jane made a little moaning sound. She didn't seem to know she was making a sound at all.

Tyl thought, *She must be in love.* Her own heart kept sinking all the time, over and over again. It would seem to swell and then fall, and the fear would come in waves. She thought, *Naturally, I don't want him to be hurt. I wouldn't want anyone to be hurt so terribly.* They rocked around the last corner and raced down a little hill to where the road led over a weighing platform and into the vast wasted-looking spaces around the city incinerator.

Jane said in Tyl's ear, "How was it that Grandy was supposed to be watching?"

Tyl said, "Because when I met him—"

"You told Grandy!"

"Of course. I—"

Jane's hand began to twist and pull. She was taking it away. She drew herself away. Tyl had the feeling that she'd been rejected. She was not included any more. The rest of this she would have to go through alone.

The taxi whizzed across the weighing platform. A man there shouted with surprise, came racing after them. They went up the ramp. The brakes screamed. They had come through the great doors and to a stop within the building. They were in a vast room—not really a room at all. The inside of this brick building was all hollow. It was nothing but a great space, enclosed by the high walls, roofed over and crossed with girders high above them, and with high windows, tilted like factory windows, some of them open, many feet up in the walls. This great space, on three sides, was empty. Echoing. Clean. But in the faintly dusty air there hung a sourish, repulsive odor.

On the fourth side were the pits. Here was where the trucks came to dump the burnable stuff. Here was where they backed up to a wooden curb and shucked off their loads. The refuse fell into huge pits built into the floor. And beyond the pits, on the other side, a great partition went up to within perhaps twenty feet of the high roof. It crossed the whole side of the building like a high parapet, with the pits like a moat in front of it.

Above it ran a kind of track from which hung a big steel-jawed bucket that was working steadily, with sullen rumblings of sound. It came down, descended into the pit, nibbled and bit at the stuff in the pits and then went up, drooling, carrying its enormous mouthful over the partition, over the wall, to some mysterious fate beyond.

Tyl looked up. Like a demon tender of the fires of hell, a head, a face with a snout, was looking down with great flat eyes, inhuman and horrible.

The human man from the weighing platform came running up behind them. They heard the howling of the siren on the police car. Grandy and Blake and the rest.

Gahagen said, "Which trucks dumped here the last half hour?" He didn't know how to put the question.

The man said, "All the trucks been in and dumped for the last time. All through."

"All of them?"

"Yeah. They get through around now. They all been in. What's wrong?"

"We don't know," Gahagen said.

Grandy and the rest came puffing up. The man who worked here was surrounded suddenly by all these visitors.

Jane, looking sick, had edged toward the pits and was looking down over the rim. Her voice pierced the dusty, rumbling emptiness of the great bare place as if it cut through a fog. "There's a trunk down there!"

"Trunk?"

"What trunk?"

"Where?"

The line of men advanced cautiously, peered over, each with one foot out, one back, with identical bendings of necks, like a line of the chorus.

"Yeah."

"Trunk, all right."

"Well?"

The employee said, "Yeah, I asked about that. Said it was full of stuff hadn't been fumigated. Typhoid. People warned them."

"When did that come in?"

"Last truck. Number Five."

Above the voices went the rumbling of the crane. Jane looked up in horror. "Stop that thing! You've got to stop it!"

"Wait a minute," said the man who worked there. "Now, listen. What's the idea? What goes on here?"

Chief Blake said, pursuing orderly thought, "Any way of finding out where they picked up that trunk?"

"Sure. Call up the yards. Get hold of the men."

"There isn't time!" cried Jane. She ducked under Chief Blake's elbow and bobbed up in front of him. "You've got to stop that thing! Stop it right now! What are you waiting for?" Her fists beat on his big blue chest. "Don't you see, if he's down there—" She was losing control.

Grandy was peering into the pit distastefully. His face was pained. The big bucket went down again, gnawed at the nauseous heap, nuzzled at it, then slowly it rose toward the top of the wall.

"Listen, they gotta clean up the pits before they can quit," the man said stubbornly. "They don't stop just for anybody's fun, you know. The men down there firing, they wanna get through."

The fires, then, must be somewhere below, somewhere below the floor where they were, and beyond that wall, at the top of which still stood the man in the gas mask. His big glassined eyes were turned down and toward them.

Fire. Very hot fire. Very hot indeed, to burn what was down there in those pits, what went slowly up in the big steel bucket, hunk by hunk, mouthful after steady mouthful.

"What a place!" said Grandy. "What a scene! What a place!" His nostrils trembled. He peered over. His hand was on Mathilda's shoulder. She shrank away from the rim, and yet something drew her irresistibly. To lean closer. To look down. She could see the top of the trunk. It was a big, old-fashioned turtleback, a big box with a humped cover. It was half buried in the debris, tilted, top upward. She tried to imagine Francis, down there in the pit, bound and imprisoned, shut in a dark box, waiting to be destroyed. She knew that was what Jane thought and imagined. But it couldn't be. It couldn't be real. Such a thing could not happen, could not be happening.

The big, empty, smelly place, the rumbling crane feeding the hidden fires, the efficiency of destruction that was going on here—the whole thing made her want to close her senses against it, not to believe, not to watch; to turn and go; to run away and go to a clean sweet place and bathe and forget.

Jane was sobbing, "Oh, please, please, listen to me! You can't take the chance! You've got to be sure!"

Grandy swayed a little. "Jane," he said, "you think he's down there!" The thought seemed to make him ill. Tyl felt him going.

She screamed. Somebody grabbed at her and held her back. She screamed again and again. The demon on the wall threw up his hands and disappeared. Men milled around her and shouted. The fumbling faltered and stopped. The bucket hung half raised, and from its iron lips the gobs of garbage fell.

Down in the pit was Grandy. He lay on his back in the ruck, his thin arms and legs spread out, his face up. Was he dead? Had he fainted? She would have gone on screaming, but the man who was holding her put his hand roughly over her mouth to stop the noise.

Jane had crouched down, was almost kneeling, right at the edge. Her eyes had a glitter. She was watching hard. Gahagen was shouting hard. Somebody came running with a rope. Gahagen was making as if to loop it around his own waist.

But Grandy wasn't dead or even unconscious. As they watched in the new silence, he struggled up. He got part way out of the ruck. Then, on his knees, he began to move, slowly, with difficulty, crawling across the pit, wallowing in the refuse because he had to, to move at all.

They heard him say, "Wait. Not yet." He was wallowing toward the trunk. He was curiously like someone swimming. He reached the trunk and hung to it a moment as if he might otherwise sink and disappear. They saw him strain to lift the lid, lift it a trifle. Saw his white head bend to bring his eyes to a position to see within.

They saw him let the lid fall, fumble a moment more as if to look again. Then he raised his arm.

They heard his voice come out of the pit, drawn out like a signal cry, humming and droning in the echoing silence, "Let . . . the ro-ope . . . do-own!"

The rope went down with a loop at the end of it Gahagen lay on the floor, looking over, calling encouragement and instruction.

Jane was a frozen bundle huddled at the brink. Her hand was flat on the dirty floor. Tyl thought, *How can she bear to get her hand so dirty*?

Somebody called out from the big entranceway, and Oliver came running across the floor. He wound up, panting, "Cop told me! Where's Grandy? Tyl, what happened?"

Tyl thought, *No time for gossip*.

"He fell."

Oliver's eyes bulged with horror.

Grandy was dangling now. They were pulling him out. He was rising from the pit on the end of the rope. They hauled him over the edge and he crumpled into a heap on the floor. His lids went down wearily.

"Fainted."

"No wonder."

"Oh, by the way, gentlemen," said Grandy's velvet voice calmly, "there's nothing in the trunk but some pieces of plaster, I think, and some old rags."

"My God, Luther, you're game!" cried Gahagen. "Good man!"

"After all," said Grandy wryly, "I was in the neighborhood." He turned his head, eyes closed, a tired old man.

Somebody laughed. Somebody swore. Somebody must have given a signal then, because the rumbling whispered out of silence, began and grew.

Oliver was kneeling at Grandy's side. He was the image of devotion. "Get a doctor," he demanded. "Get an ambulance."

"Nonsense, my dear boy," said Grandy, but his lids were trembling. He looked very sick. He was filthy and contaminated—fastidious Grandy! An old man, after all. He lay on the dirty floor.

"This'll be the end of him!" cried Oliver in despair. "Call a doctor, one of you! Hurry, can't you see? Tyl, snap out of it"

Tyl stood looking on. She had not fallen on her knees. She felt unable to bend or to move at all. She contemplated the image of devotion. She saw the puppet working to swing attention and concern. She saw Grandy lying filthy on the floor and the people all beginning to swing, to center him.

The scene had nothing to do with her. She was alone, outside the circle and alone, suspended, lost. A puppet without strings would be as limp and lost. The bucket descended, to fall again at its work. She noticed that it had a weakness. She felt it was curiously repulsive that the great wicked thing with its greedy mouth was so weak at the neck. It had no neck, only cables. It fell weakly, and then it would nibble and chew and scrabble about, and gape and close and rise sternly, with the cable taut, to carry its load over the wall. Mathilda's eyes followed it.

Jane wasn't in the circle, either. That circle around Grandy, where invisible bands drew like elastic, where he was pulling them with the magnet of himself, and they were responding like iron filings.

Jane screamed. Jane got up from the crouching position and fastened on Blake's arm. "No, stop it! Don't let it start! You've got to look!"

"Look where, Miss?"

"In the trunk! In the trunk!"

"Mr. Grandison looked." The big arm rejected her.

"No, no, not Mr. Grandison! You can't trust him!"

"What do you mean, you can't trust—"

Oliver got up. "What the devil's the matter with you, Jane?" he asked severely.

"Francis is in that trunk! In a minute that thing is going to take it! Where does it take things? Where does it go?"

"The chutes. To the fires," somebody said.

"No!" Jane was nearly hysterical. "I tell you, you can't take his word! Any one man's word! You've got to stop that thing! Open the trunk! Let me see! Let me see inside!"

"Now, just a minute, miss. After all—"

"It's your duty!" she cried. Tears ran down her face. She was frantic.

Oliver said, "Slap her, somebody. Slap her in the face." His voice got shrill. "We've got to get Grandy out of here! He's a mess! Tyl!"

"Seems to me we've done our duty," Blake was answering. "Mr. Grandison saw what was inside the trunk. Now, miss—er—you don't know the trunk came from Press's house, do you? It could have come from anywhere in town. It's full of typhoid germs."

Tyl thought dully, *Grandy'll catch typhoid.* She was watching the bucket, on its way up now. It seemed to be working a little faster. The men who tended the fires wanted to get through and get home.

Jane said, "I know I can't make you believe he's lying. But he could be mistaken. You can't afford to take even that chance. Suppose he's mistaken? It's a man's life! Mathilda knows he was there in that house."

Tyl stirred. "Yes," she said dully. She thought, *If I can trust my own senses.*

The bucket was dropping down. Its cables were slack. It fell with that disgusting weakness at the neck. It fell, it nibbled, it crept quite near. Quite near the old turtleback trunk that lay half buried.

The bucket's jaws were big enough to take it up—just about big enough. Perhaps next time.

". . . nobody in the cellar."

". . . girl musta made a mistake."

Blake said impatiently, "Now, look, miss. If I thought there was any danger—"

"I don't care what you think! I know there's danger!"

Oliver said, "What's this about, anyhow? I wish somebody would—"

Jane said, "Don't take the time to tell him."

Maddeningly, Blake began, "This young lady—"

"Stop that thing, I tell you!" Jane's voice was ugly with her terror. "Stop it!" She tore her throat with the cry.

Gahagen said, "Aren't you a little bit hysterical?"

Oliver said, "For God's sake, with Grandy maybe dying—"

Grandy was just lying there, pale and wan, filthy, done in, so weary and ill and pathetic.

Jane's eyes turned in her head to catch sight of the bucket going up. Not yet had it got the trunk into its jaws.

Mathilda was alone. She knew they were all gathered around Grandy, who lay so dramatically exhausted at their feet. She could hear voices talking, talking, and Jane arguing, reasoning, pleading. And the bucket was coming down again.

She heard Jane cry, "Somebody help me! . . . Mathilda, help me!"

One would have to answer such a cry.

But Grandy stirred, and she heard his voice, "Where's Tyl?" It carried through every other noise, that beloved voice, so rich and tender. "Where's my duckling?" he said. He called her to him. "Is she all right?" That was his anxious love. "Tyl, darling."

Mathilda's head turned. His hand was out, waiting for hers to slide within it. Appealing to her. Confident of her. His darling. Yes, of course, she was his darling.

She saw something on the floor. It was as if there was an explosion inside her head.

She gasped, put out her hand. "Oh, please . . . please." The words rose out of her throat to join Jane's. Then she thought, *Talk, words. Words won't do it. What's the use of talking*? For Jane had been talking; Jane was still begging them, weeping, pleading. But Grandy, lying on the floor with his eyes shut, was too strong.

Mathilda's body was taut now, and it felt strong and alive. Leaning a little forward, she said, quietly, aloud, "If Francis is down there, it's got to stop."

She flung up her arms. For a second she was poised in the air, a Winged Victory indeed. Then she had done it. She was falling, falling. She struck the soft, rotten, evil heap. She had leaped. She was down in the pit.

Above, men were shouting again.

Oh, yes, now the bucket would not come down. Mathilda smiled. She'd stopped it. She'd stopped it quickly the only way. In a moment or two, she straggled up and began to wade, as Grandy had done. She toiled and struggled. It was nightmarish, that journey through the evil muck. Her hand reached the trunk, touched its hard surfaces. Both hands now were at the lock.

From above, they saw what she was trying to do, and they saw her fail. They heard her when she called to them. Heard her cry when she said, "I can't! The trunk's locked! It's locked!"

"Locked?"

Gahagen looked at Blake, and he looked down where Grandy lay, rolled on his side now, peering over. Grandy's big, thick-knuckled hand on the curb, the rim of the pit, tightened, loosened.

Down in the pit, where the fumes rose and overpowered her, Mathilda fainted.

33

Mathilda was bathed, scrubbed, scented and immaculate. She lay on the couch by the fire, wearing a coral-colored frock. Her legs were lovely in her best sheer prewar stockings. Her feet were comfortable in gold kid mules. Her hair had been washed and brushed until it shone. It was tied back with a coral ribbon. She looked very young and a little pale.

Jane was sitting on the little low-backed chair, the skirt of her brown dirndl spread around her. A bracelet slid on her arm where she propped up her chin. Oliver was back a little, with his face in shadow.

These three were silent, listening to what Tom Gahagen and Francis were saying, trying not to think about what had happened to Grandy. Grandy was dead.

It was not yet certain whether or not from natural causes, whether his arrogant spirit had arrogantly fled from the prospect of disgrace by some hocus-pocus of his own will and device, perhaps by poison, or whether an old man's heart had been unable to stand the various excitements and had literally broken.

Anyhow, he was dead. There would be no legal aftermath. No long-drawn-out, sensational trial. It was all over really. Except the chase after Press and his wife. They would be caught and explode into headlines. Yes, it was all over but the headlines. And they, too, would pass.

Francis was not only alive and well, but looking extremely handsome in a soft blue country-style shirt without any tie. Shaved. Shampooed. His hair looked crisp and still damp.

They were, perhaps, the cleanest group of people gathered anywhere at that given moment. Mathilda had the thought. But she didn't smile. Her whole heart ached. Pale and quiet, she lay, and although she listened, something inside kept weeping, not for the shell of Grandy, who lay somewhere in the town, but for the Grandy who had never lived at all, for the Grandy that never was, the one she'd loved.

With the one she'd loved went everything she'd known. All gone. She could not yet be sure what anyone was, what anything was like. She'd seen the world through Grandy's eyes. That world was gone. Even his chair they'd pushed away. The long room was his no more. It was a strange room in a strange house where she'd always been a stranger.

Gahagen said, "He never made as much money in the theater as people thought. You see what he did? The head of the firm that handled the estate for Frazier, he died. So Grandy got into disagreement with the juniors and took the business away. So there was nearly two years when the fortune was fluid, and Grandy was handling things himself, buying, selling, changing things around. While he had everything confused, he must have managed to transfer a pretty big hunk of the stuff into his own name. Then he gave the business to a new firm. How would they know she'd been robbed? But I can't figure out how you ever got on the track of such a thing from the outside."

"Jane had a letter," said Francis. His dark eyes were somber and troubled. "It was little Rosaleen Wright who got on to it."

Mathilda's heart ached.

"I don't suppose we'll ever know exactly how," said Francis in that sad, patient way. "But she was here when Mathilda turned twenty-one and made her will. Maybe then—"

Mathilda said, "They did work on it a long time, the lawyer and Rosaleen. He wouldn't."

"Grandy wouldn't?" Somebody said the name she couldn't say.

"He said financial matters were too dull. He said it was a paper world." She turned her face to the inside of the couch.

"Maybe Rosaleen wondered why the records didn't go all the way back to your father's death," said Gahagen.

"She wouldn't have been fooled," said Jane suddenly. "There was something terribly honest about Rosaleen."

"You knew her well?" said Gahagen sympathetically.

"She was my cousin," Jane said. "We all grew up next door to each other."

"You never did think she killed herself?"

"No," said Jane. "And now I can imagine how he did it. I can imagine how he'd have asked her to write out that suicide note. He'd have made it seem plausible. He'd have—"

Mathilda closed her eyes.

Jane's voice was a knife.

"—maybe said to her, 'I'm experimenting, dear child.' There'd be that hook up in the ceiling. He'd have said he was trying to understand one of his old crimes. He could have got everything ready right under her eyes, because he'd have been talking, the way he talked, all the time."

Mathilda shuddered. The spell was broken. She could see now that he'd been a spellbinder. She could feel a shadow of the spell.

Oliver said, with a whine in his voice, "I wish you people had come to me. I could have helped you. Althea did tell me about that

'Burn tenderly' business. I was your missing witness, if you'd only known. I didn't know that you needed a witness. We just didn't get together."

Francis said gently, "None of you could be expected to see our point of view." He didn't say it reproachfully, but as if the fact had been troublesome, but not misunderstood.

Oliver said weakly, "I suppose that's so."

Gahagen turned curiously to Mathilda. "But you finally did see their point of view, Miss Tyl. What made you so sure, all of a sudden?"

She felt blank and dull, couldn't remember.

"Up to that point, you were pretty near ready to think you'd been seeing things, weren't you? I don't understand how you came to be sure enough to take a jump like that."

Mathilda said, slowly, "I don't know. Yes, I do, but I don't know how to explain it exactly."

"Don't try," said Francis quickly.

"Oh, yes," she said, "I'll try." She went on, groping. "You see, there were a lot of pieces. I'd heard all about the fuse blowing. Oliver gave me another piece. He told me how Althea had heard a man on the radio. Then Jane gave me another piece when she said she'd been checking up, and the man had said 'Burn tenderly' so late that morning. You see, I had all the pieces. They went together, just all of a sudden."

They sighed.

"But that wasn't all," Tyl said more vigorously. She felt better for being able to explain. "There was another handful of pieces. You see, I knew Francis had been down in the cellar." She was half sitting up now, her face was vivid. "And I was sure it was Francis, on account of the candy. Who else could have left that for me to see?"

"Who else but you could have seen it?" said Francis huskily.

"Well"—she shot him a green glance—"then Jane had her story

about the man Mr. Press and the truck. I just suddenly saw that if Grandy wasn't"—she'd said the name —"wasn't a true link, if he was unreliable, then the impossibilities all cleared up. I just suddenly put the thing together and I saw that Francis had been there. He had gone; he must have gone somewhere, and Jane was on the track of how he could have gone. And then," she said, "I happened to look at Grandy, and I saw that piece of Dutch chocolate spilling out of his trousers pocket."

"The candy?"

"Yes." A little shiver ran down her slim body. "I didn't stop to think he might have had one of his own chocolates in his pocket. I just remembered that I'd seen them on the ground by that house, and that they'd disappeared. Who picked them up? If I wasn't crazy— Who knew enough to pick them up? Who knew what they meant? Only me, and Francis . . . and Grandy.

"So you see," she added quietly, "I understood that he wasn't reliable. I think I just . . . saw him."

"He was—" Gahagen shook his head. He had no adjective for what Grandy had been. "Then, when he unlocked that trunk under our noses to pretend to look inside! And he locked it again too. He didn't dare risk the thing falling open when the bucket picked it up. Of course, that finished him."

"You were quick to see that," Jane praised him.

Francis said, "I must say I'm glad I was out like a light most of that time. I'm just as pleased I didn't know about that bucket or where I was."

Jane said simply, "I nearly went crazy."

Mathilda, looking at the pulse in Francis' throat, thought, *So did I.*

"Well, that finished him," said Francis abruptly. "He might have pleaded bad eyesight. He just might have been able to pretend he couldn't distinguish me from a bunch of old rags in the bad light, eh? He'd have talked, and who's to say he might not have wriggled out of it, when and if you'd found my bones? But with that key in his pocket!"

"He fell in on purpose, to keep us from looking inside that trunk," said Gahagen. "It was a brilliant idea. Mr. Howard, here, might have been pretty well destroyed. We might not even have stopped the works to look again. I don't know. Can't say. Looking back, it seems impossible that we believed him at all. But, of course, we did believe him at the time."

Gahagen got up to go. Perhaps his tongue slipped. When he said "Good night," he called Mathilda "Mrs. Howard."

When he had gone, Francis moved restlessly about, poked at the fire.

Oliver came out of the shadows and took a nearer chair. "Doesn't he know you two aren't married?" he asked with bright interest.

Francis stood still, with the poker in his hand swinging like a pendulum. "I guess you realize now that Grandy deliberately rearranged your wedding," he said bluntly.

Whose wedding? What was he talking about? Tyl looked up. Met his eye. "Mine!" she gasped.

Oliver said, "Ours, dear."

Tyl let her head fall back again. She didn't know how revealing her face was. How its serenity and the simple curiosity with which she asked her question told them so much. "But why didn't he want Oliver and me to marry?" she wondered almost placidly.

"He didn't want you to marry, ever," said Francis angrily, "on account of the money. Didn't he teach you to think you'd never be loved except for the money? Didn't he make you believe you weren't personally very attractive? Didn't he play up Althea against you? Weren't you always the Ugly Duckling? And not a damn word of it true." He put the poker into its place with a banging of metal on metal. Mathilda felt surprised.

Oliver said uneasily, "He certainly tried—"

"Of course he was a pretty persuasive old bird," said Francis much more mildly.

Oliver's face was red. Of course, thought Mathilda. Oliver had let Grandy persuade him. He hadn't seen Mathilda or Althea either with his own eyes, but through Grandy's eyes. And now Oliver was ashamed. So now he was preparing to laugh it off. Oliver was about to be nonchalant. How well she knew all the silly expressions on his silly face.

"Mathilda doesn't care for me," said Oliver gaily. "Maybe I'll marry Jane."

"I don't think so," said Jane promptly. "My husband wouldn't like it."

Francis laughed and got up and put his arms around Jane. He put his chin down on her hair. "You're wonderful," he said. "Little old Jane." He kissed her. "Go to bed now. I want to talk to Mathilda."

When Jane had gone and Oliver had, rather awkwardly, gone, too, and they were alone, Francis' eyes were filled again with trouble. But Mathilda's green eyes were wide open now. The long room was a real room, after all. Those people were real. She could see.

She said, "I thought you were engaged to Rosaleen?"

"I was."

"But . . . you're married to Jane!"

He gasped. "I'm not married to Jane. Her husband happens to be in Hawaii at the moment. That's Buddy." He began to laugh. "It's ridiculous, but she's my little old Aunt Jane. My father's youngest sister, bringing up the rear of the family. Hasn't anyone told you? I'm Francis Moynihan."

"Oh." Mathilda played with her belt. She said, "I haven't seen things or people the way they are. It's hard to begin to see."

He said, "I know." He said, "But you'll be all right." He said, "You need to . . . look around now. Now that he's gone."

She turned her face away. Her heart—something—ached terribly.

He said, "I realize how you see me. I don't know how to explain to you or apologize. I dreamed up this thing before I knew you. In fact, I thought you were dead."

She murmured that she wasn't.

"I know," he said. He got up again and ran his fingers through his hair. He didn't seem to know how to go on.

She lifted her head. "But who is that Doctor White?"

He corrected her gently, "Doctor Wright. Rosaleen's father."

"Oh. Oh, then that's why— He walks like Rosaleen."

"Does he? Yes, I guess he does."

Francis looked unhappily into the fire. "What can I do now about this marriage business?" he blurted. "You see, I haven't told. Gahagen doesn't know. The papers will say I stumbled on something suspicious after I got here. I didn't want you dragged through all that—at least until I asked you what you wanted."

She said nothing. She thought, *Is it up to me*?

"Tyl, what can I do now to fix things? Would you like to get a—fake divorce? That might be better for you. Better than to confess all this ridiculous masquerade. What do you think?"

"Can we get a divorce if we're not really married?" she asked thoughtfully.

"Maybe we can fake something."

"Let's not fake any more," she murmured. "Do you think Doctor Wright would just quietly marry us—really, I mean?"

"Tyl—" He half crossed the rug to her, but he stopped.

Her green eyes were wide open and cool. “Then, you see, the divorce could follow.”

“I see.” He went back to poke at the fire. He ran his fingers through his hair. He took a turn on the hearth rug. Then he looked at her and his brows flew up. “It’s a risk,” he warned.

“Risk?” she repeated.

“Terrible risk.”

She got up on her elbow and looked across at him with a curious intentness, as if she were, indeed, seeing him for the first time. “I don’t think so,” she said slowly.

He came quickly to her and sat on the edge of her couch. He took her hands. “We’ll do that, if it’s what you think will be— Actually, it might be the sensible way. There’s no risk, Mathilda.”

“You don’t mind?” she murmured.

He said with a twist of his mouth, “Why, I guess the rest of my life is yours. There’s no one else I owe it to.”

She shook her head, not satisfied.

His eyes lit, but he hid the light. “We’ll do that, Tyl,” he murmured. “Then . . . we’ll see.”

She nodded. He put his face down on her hands.

OTTO PENZLER PRESENTS

AMERICAN MYSTERY CLASSICS

Erle Stanley Gardner

The Case of the Careless Kitten

Introduction by Otto Penzler

Perry Mason seeks the link between a poisoned kitten and a mysterious voice from the past

Soon after Helen Kendal receives a mysterious phone call from her vanished uncle Franklin, long presumed dead, urging her to make contact with criminal defense attorney Perry Mason, she finds herself the main suspect in the murder of an unfamiliar man. Her kitten has just survived a poisoning attempt—as has her aunt Matilda, who always maintained that Franklin was alive in spite of his disappearance. Certain of his client's innocence, Mason gets to work outwitting the police to solve the crime; to do so, he'll enlist the help of his secretary Della Street, his private eye Paul Drake, and the unlikely but invaluable aid of a careless but very clever kitten.

Erle Stanley Gardner (1889-1970) was the best-selling American author of the 20th century, mainly due to the enormous success of his Perry Mason series. For more than a quarter of a century he wrote more than a million words a year under his own name and numerous pseudonyms, the most famous being A.A. Fair. His series books can be read in any order.

"[Erle Stanley Gardner's] Mason books remain tantalizing on every page and brilliant."
—Scott Turow

Paperback, $15.95 / ISBN 978-1-61316-116-6
Hardcover, $25.95 / ISBN 978-1-61316-115-9

OTTO PENZLER PRESENTS

AMERICAN MYSTERY CLASSICS

H.F. Heard

A Taste for Honey

Introduction by Otto Penzler

In the English countryside, a recluse and a beekeeper team up to catch a cunning villain

In a quiet village far from the noise of London, Sydney Silchester lives the life of a recluse led by two passions: privacy and honey. He gives up the former only when his stores of the latter run low. But when his honey supplier is found stung to death by her hive, the search for a new beekeeper takes Sydney to Mr. Mycroft, a brilliant man who has retired to Sussex to take up precisely this occupation (and who shares many traits with the great detective, Sherlock Holmes). Upon hearing of the tragic death of the village's other beekeeper, Mycroft immediately senses the bloody hand of murder. But what villain would have the mad intelligence to train an army of killer bees? Together, the reluctant duo embark on a life-threatening search for the perpetrator of this most diabolical crime.

H.F. Heard (1889-1971) was an English author renowned for his writings on religious, historical, and mystical subjects, published under the name Gerald Heard. He moved to the United States in 1937, after which point he published several mystery novels, even while continuing his spiritual work that included his founding a meditation center in the Southwest.

"A very clever thriller."
—Raymond Chandler

Paperback, $15.95 / ISBN 978-1-61316-121-0

Hardcover, $25.95 / ISBN 978-1-61316-120-3

OTTO PENZLER PRESENTS

AMERICAN MYSTERY CLASSICS

Stuart Palmer

The Puzzle of the Happy Hooligan

Introduction by Otto Penzler

After a screenwriter is murdered on a film set, a street-smart school teacher searches for the killer

Hildegarde Withers is just your average school teacher—with above-average skills in the art of deduction. The New Yorker often finds herself investigating crimes led only by her own meddlesome curiosity, though her friends on the NYPD don't mind when she solves their cases for them. After plans for a grand tour of Europe are interrupted by Germany's invasion of Poland, Miss Withers heads to sunny Los Angeles instead, where her vacation finds her working as a technical advisor on the set of a film adaptation of the Lizzie Borden story. The producer has plans for an epic retelling of the historical killer's patricidal spree—plans which are derailed when a screenwriter turns up dead. While the local authorities quickly deem his death accidental, Withers suspects otherwise and calls up a detective back home for advice. The two soon team up to catch a wily killer.

Stuart Palmer (1905–1968) was an American author of mysteries. Born in Baraboo, Wisconsin, Palmer worked a number of odd jobs—including apple picking, journalism, and copywriting—before publishing his first novel, the crime drama *Ace of Jades*, in 1931.

"Will keep you laughing and guessing from the first page to the last."—*The New York Times*

Paperback, $15.95 / ISBN 978-1-61316-104-3

Hardcover, $25.95 / ISBN 978-1-61316-114-2

OTTO PENZLER PRESENTS

AMERICAN MYSTERY CLASSICS

Patrick Quentin
A Puzzle for Fools
Introduction by Otto Penzler

A wave of murders rocks a sanitarium —and it's up to the patients to stop them

Broadway producer Peter Duluth sought solace in a bottle after his wife's death; now, two years later and desperate to dry out, he enters a sanitarium, hoping to break his dependence on drink—but the institution doesn't quite offer the rest and relaxation he expected. Strange, malevolent occurrences plague the hospital; among other inexplicable events, Peter hears his own voice with an ominous warning: "There will be murder." It soon becomes clear that a homicidal maniac is on the loose and, with a staff every bit as erratic as its idiosyncratic patients, it seems everyone is a suspect—even Duluth's new romantic interest, Iris Pattison. Charged by the head of the ward with solving the crimes, it's up to Peter to clear her name before the killer strikes again.

PATRICK QUENTIN is one pseudonym of Hugh Callingham Wheeler (1912-1987), born in London, who eventually became a US citizen. Writing in collaboration with a revolving cast of co-authors under the Quentin, Q. Patrick and Jonathan Stagge names, Wheeler produced more than 30 mystery novels. He later gravitated to the stage and wrote, among other plays, the Tony Award-winning *Sweeney Todd.*

"Mr. Quentin is a craftsman of the first class."
—*Times Literary Supplement*

Paperback, $15.95 / ISBN 978-1-61316-125-8

Hardcover, $25.95 / ISBN 978-1-61316-124-1

OTTO PENZLER PRESENTS
AMERICAN MYSTERY CLASSICS

Craig Rice
Home Sweet Homicide
Introduction by Otto Penzler

The children of a mystery writer play amateur sleuths and matchmakers

Unoccupied and unsupervised while mother is working, the children of widowed crime writer Marion Carstairs find diversion wherever they can. So when the kids hear gunshots at the house next door, they jump at the chance to launch their own amateur investigation—and after all, why shouldn't they? They know everything the cops do about crime scenes, having read about them in mother's novels. They know what her literary detectives would do in such a situation, how they would interpret the clues and handle witnesses. Plus, if the children solve the puzzle before the cops, it will do wonders for the sales of mother's novels. But this crime scene isn't a game at all; the murder is real and, when its details prove more twisted than anything in mother's fiction, they'll eventually have to enlist Marion's help to sort out the clues. Or is that just part of their plan to hook her up with the lead detective on the case?

Craig Rice (1908–1957), born Georgiana Ann Randolph Craig, was an American author of mystery novels, short stories, and screenplays. Rice's writing style was unique in its ability to mix gritty, hard-boiled writing with the entertainment of a screwball comedy.

"A genuine midcentury classic."—*Booklist*

Paperback, $15.95 / ISBN 978-1-61316-103-6

Hardcover, $25.95 / ISBN 978-1-61316-112-8